It is 1937, and Europe is on the brink of war. Hitler is circulating a most-wanted list of "cultural degenerates"—artists, writers, and thinkers whose work is deemed antithetical to the new regime. To prevent the destruction of her favorite art (and artists), the impetuous American heiress and modern art collector Leonora Calaway begins chartering boats and planes for an elite group of surrealists to Costalegre, a mysterious resort in the Mexican jungle.

The story of what happens to these artists when they reach their destination is told from the point of view of Lara, Leonora's neglected fifteen-year-old daughter. Forced from a young age to live with her mother's eccentric whims, tortured lovers, and entourage of gold-diggers, Lara suffers from emotional, educational, and geographical instability that a Mexican sojourn with surrealists isn't going to help. But when she meets the outcast Dadaist sculptor Jack Klinger, Lara thinks she might have found the love and understanding she so badly craves.

Sinuous and striking, heartbreaking and strange, *Costalegre* is inspired by the real-life relationship between the heiress Peggy Guggenheim and her daughter Pegeen. Courtney Maum triumphs with this wildly imaginative and curiously touching story of a privileged teenager who has everything a girl could wish for—except a mother who loves her back.

"When young Lara finds herself in Costalegre, living with her mother and a gaggle of twentieth-century surrealist artists, wonder and mayhem ensue. With this slim novel, Courtney Maum has gifted her readers with a breathtaking meditation on youth, art, and the ever-mysterious bonds between mothers and daughters. *Costalegre* is a spectacular high-wire act that dazzles and devastates."

—LAURA VAN DEN BERG, author of *The Third Hotel*

"Mesmerizing and unsettling, *Costalegre* is a wonder, and Courtney Maum shows herself once again to be a writer of many gifts. This is a book for anyone who's ever loved, and not felt sufficiently loved in return; and for anyone who's had to try to grow up; for, that is, everyone."

—R.O. KWON, author of *The Incendiaries*

"Here is war and here is art. And here is a child trying to become an adult in the midst of a Mexican exile. Maum's stirred a brew of careless bohemians, Führers and failed art students, negligent mothers and missing museums. *Costalegre* is as heady, delirious, and heartbreaking as a young girl just beginning to fall in love with the world."

—SAMANTHA HUNT, author of *The Dark Dark*

"Courtney Maum's *Costalegre* is a marvel—so lively, intimate, and strange, you don't read so much as dream the voice and visions of Lara, our fifteen-year-old narrator, writing from a house full of surrealists in Mexico as they wait out WWII. This is a special book, by a writer who proves on these pages that she can do anything."

—**JULIE BUNTIN**, author of *Marlena*

"This story of a daughter searching for connection all around her has a sharp cutting edge, a world which changes its mood in an instant; bleak as the dregs of a wine-soaked dinner, then bullish as a house of hapless surrealists attempting to boil an egg. Memorable and meaningful, *Costalegre* remains with me as a reminder of love in the agony of teenage years and art in the terror of war."

—**AMELIA GRAY**, author of *Isadora*

"In this story where our fifteen-year-old narrator is more mature and intuitive than the adult artists who surround her, bursts of brilliance hit me—chapter after chapter—like waves crashing against the shores of this allegorical Mexican coast. With its captivating mix of true-to-life characters and WWII history, *Costalegre* is surreal, intelligent, and full of integrity."

—**MARK EISNER**, author of *Neruda: The Biography of a Poet*

Copyright © 2019 Courtney Maum

Published by Tin House Books, Portland, Oregon

Distributed by W. W. Norton & Company

Library of Congress Cataloging-in-Publication Data

Names: Maum, Courtney, 1978- author.
Title: Costalegre / Courtney Maum.
Description: First U.S. edition. | Portland, Oregon : Tin House Books, 2019.
Identifiers: LCCN 2019005789 | ISBN 9781947793361 (hardcover)
Classification: LCC PS3613.A87396 C67 2019 | DDC 813/.6--dc23
LC record available at https://lccn.loc.gov/2019005789

Printed in the USA
Interior design: Diane Chonette
Interior illustrations: © Dasha Ziborova
www.tinhouse.com

COSTALEGRE

COURTNEY MAUM

 TIN HOUSE BOOKS / Portland, Oregon

For the daughters

Les bois sont blancs ou noirs,
on ne dormira jamais.

—ANDRÉ BRETON, 1924

1937

Sábado

Mother's brought them all this time—the entire bin of loons. Already, nails and hammers. Rags drying in the trees.

The way over was days long, my clothing sticking to me, our bags chalked because mother never tips. She and her awful vulture man holding court in the dayroom. Endless speculation and the sharp sound of cracked ice. Hetty, even more desperate than usual, telling Mumma not to drink so much, that we were at such an altitude, and with all the bumps . . . but it was of course Hetty who was sick first, and into a paper bag which was one of those cheerful bags that is sharp in the corners and just the right size, and there would have been so many other nicer uses for that bag.

A fueling stop in the Azores. We sat (and sat) in the cafés. The Portuguese authorities went through all our trunks and letters without any idea, I don't think, of what they were looking for. Mostly, they wanted news from France, but their French was very bad and their English, entertaining. Konrad told them the Führer was coming but he hadn't arrived yet, and Mum bought a straw hat.

I really liked the sleeping berths and was assigned one of my own, but of course, Konrad can't be forced to sleep with Mumma in such small quarters, so I was forced to share with her, which was—as it always is—moist. She has always been a noisy sleeper but her botched nose makes it worse, and plus, there was the sound of the engines and the propellers slashing through the night. Except for the views, which are dreamlike, as if you're finally a bird, it's terrible to throttle through the space and sky.

All the other loonies are coming on a boat, and I spent a lot of time scanning the ocean for them. For a pirate ship. That's what they should be on, really, a lively pirate ship. Mum told me the artists would be held for ages at customs and that it was silly to look for them when I could play a game with the ones we already had, but it didn't seem that farfetched to imagine one of the Spaniards floating calmly on a canvas or flying on some swan. And in any case, I did see boats, a lot of them. Just not the ones my mother had paid to help escape.

Hetty was sick again, by the way, on the drive out to Costalegre. Not that I can blame her (the drive is from a nightmare), but I will blame her all the same. She is just so nervous and muttering incessantly about how it will be too hot to write, and I want to say that no one would have minded if she'd stayed in France.

But the heat is something that will stay with me forever. In any case, it's too disheartening to describe the bus ride, which seemed longer and hotter and more . . . reptilian than it did when I was seven, the last time we were here. There were so few of us then, just Mumma and me, and Papa, a tutor for me and Stephan (and Stephan also there), and Magda, who loved me, who Mum says she couldn't find to cook for us this year. Of course there were artists. There are always artists. But I remember them as friendly and they didn't live in our same house.

Now Mum says that I can't count on finding Magda and that what with all of the urgency around our leaving, she couldn't find a tutor for me either. And who knows how long we will be in Mexico! Meanwhile, Steph gets to stay in school and go round honking on his alphorn while I'm carted through the jungle with all of Mum's rescues. If she ends up putting her museum here, I am going to die.

Sábado, later

So I have a new father. His name is Konrad Beck and he
hates Mumma more than Papa did. He is tall and narrow
but quite tan for a German. He was in an internment
camp so he is thin and angry. Mum saved him by marry-
ing him—he is the toast of all the town! So of course
Legrand is jealous, Legrand who really is a vulture, and
just as indiscreet. Legrand says Konrad is the most
important surrealist in all of Europe, after him.

Konrad is in love with a beautiful woman named C., so
Mum brought her along, also. Charlotte is a famous writer
but because she is a woman, I guess she goes by C. There
is talk of all the horses they will ride. Mother's furious—
she can't ride anymore because of the problems with her
ankles, but we rode when we were here last—the beaches
are beautiful and the sand is deep and wet, which makes
it harder for the horses to run away with you. I know Mum
is wretched about these plans because she won't be able to

follow them—I've heard that C. is very good. But she'll still check their hair when they get back to see if they went swimming, that's what she did with us.

There's not much that Mum can do about C. She is beautiful and talented and also she's from England, and Mum's jealous to death about her accent and her pretty skin. C. wears thick white shirts tucked into long navy skirts of the same material, and somehow she keeps them clean, and of course the contrast is very painful with mother, who is always changing outfits to suit her mood. I understand why Konrad loves C. I think it is hard not to. But still, Mumma would be so much calmer if Konrad acted thankfully.

Hetty is the only other woman with us in Mexico, besides Mum and C. As I have mentioned, Hetty is just horrible. She's so persistent, she's like a dripping nose. Hetty is also a writer, and is terrifically jealous of C., who has published several books already and always to high praise. Mostly, though, Hetty is Mum's secretary and her minder, in a way. She's always running after her trying to get her to drink more water, and me, to get more sun. But not too much because Mumma likes my hair golden but not yellow—I'm telling you, she's the worst. She hates Konrad because he doesn't love my mother and she can't stand Legrand because he thinks she doesn't have a light on in her head. This is probably the only thing I agree on with Legrand! Hetty wishes that mother listened to her the way she heeds Legrand, but my mother doesn't know what to do with other women except try to dress like them.

Anyway, we're not in the same house as last time, which was beautiful, and pink. It was small and perched above the ocean next to a row of other *casitas*, but this time, we have one of the *casas*, and we are all alone. The place is called Occidente and it's the brightest blue. It's right above Teopa Beach so actually Mum probably can watch them go horse riding and ring a bell or something if they swim.

Legrand was the one who assigned everyone to rooms, which of course Hetty was upset about, because he gave her the worst one. I'm on the third floor with the rock collector and the photographer, and Baldomero was given his own house. Mum is on the second floor near Legrand, whose room is almost as big as hers. My room is circular, even the bed is circular, and there is just a piece of fabric instead of a real door. There is also a giant hole cut out of the wall that looks onto the sea. It's supposed to be the *ojo*, the eye they put in all the bedrooms here. Well, it's creepy to think the boats out there can see into my room.

I've brought along my art supplies and of course I have this diary, but other than writing and painting and looking nice for Mumma, it's unclear what I'm supposed to do. Mum says when we settle in, she'll see about a tutor, but she doesn't speak Spanish, so how will she do that?

She said she thought I should take lessons from the other artists in their proper disciplines, and that if I did that, I would be a cultured girl. But what am I going to learn? How to be upset with everything and turn things upside down?

Mum says our artists are the ones the Führer decided were the most degenerate in Europe and that they couldn't stay there if they kept making art like that. Konrad has actually met the Führer and says that the entire thing is because the Führer is a terrible artist so he's jealous of the good ones. They were in art school together and the Führer was always doing landscapes, so now he thinks all German people should only do landscapes too. Konrad told my mother Europe will go to war over bad watercolors. It was so nice to hear them laugh.

<u>What I'm not happy about:</u>
The heat!
Not being able to/not knowing how to swim
Antoine Legrand
Hetty!
War!

<u>What I'm happy about:</u>
Having time with Mumma
The rock collector can maybe teach me sign language
Making some new paintings
C.
Not being in stupid France
My hair
Maybe Stephan and Papa will join us if the war gets bad

Martes

Last night at dinner, there was a fight about whether or not to keep the staff. They are here year-round. We haven't come in seven years but they stay on just in case, sweeping petals from the courtyard and pushing wire brushes across the droppings left by bats. Except for Magda, as I've mentioned, who Mum says can't be found. And I can't even ask the other Mexicans about her because I don't speak Spanish and there is no way I'm asking Baldomero to speak to them for me because he would think it hysterical to say something I hadn't actually asked.

In Costalegre the male servers wear white with red boleros and the girls wear these fetching shift dresses with flowers and birds embroidered on them in red, yellow, and green. Way down below the house, you can see the wet dresses flapping in the sun. You wouldn't believe how quickly they go dry. You have to be fast about it, can't leave them all day there: the colors lose their colors in the sun.

We started with cold soup and everyone was quiet while they served it. The soup made a glucky sound as it was spooned into the bowls, and the French photographer, Caspar, got some on his shirt. It was the serving girl's fault, but you would have thought the worst had happened, with how upset he was. Caspar hates it here, he'll probably hate it always. If I had to go everywhere with Baldomero, I would hate it too. (It was Baldomero who brought him. He wants a pet kinkajou and he wants Caspar to take photographs of them together when he finds it.)

When the servants returned to the kitchen, Hetty said wasn't it just something, the lovely darkness of their skin, and Legrand went into a huff as he is wont to do when Hetty opens up her mouth.

"I told you to do away with servants!" is what Legrand said. He doesn't believe in having servants. Says it makes him self-conscious about his art.

Mum went on with the soup-eating. "Life would be impossible without them. You have no idea what the road is like to get food."

New papa was eating glumly, as he usually does. "Our colleagues are starving. And we're being served soup."

Mother snapped up, and it started. Actually, it's not a snap, when she gets going; it's slow and cool and all the more frightening for its coolness and its slowness.

"Your colleagues are not starving," she said, scoop of spoon, a slurp. "They're in second-class cabins cavorting in some social hall on top of the Atlantic. Hardly a great hardship, I should say. And in any case"—the spoon was put to rest, and I'd forgotten breathing—"the staff comes with the house."

They come with the house, and they go with the house too. I thought of the people left behind in Paris, all of the staff there. Henri the driver, not brought because he'd have nothing to drive here, and the girl in her ironed navy uniform who never looked at me, because we're the same age.

"Open the prisons! Disband the armies! Bring them to our table!" Legrand roared.

Mother sighed here, and so I shall make proof of it: she doesn't always love him. Hetty was stricken with panic. C. worked through the wine.

C.—"Perhaps if there weren't so many, is the thing."

Caspar (who had returned from the kitchen, a wet patch on his breast)— "It's despicable. Being served."

Mum—"Really, I think you'd all be far more uncomfortable if you had to share your meal with staff. What, will Baldomero translate?"

Baldomero—"I, for one, find it positively luscious to be served."

Konrad—"Perhaps you dine alone, then. In your tower . . ."

Legrand—"We are Europeans. Surely we can cook."

Mum—"I'm an American. And I can't. You can send the staff away as far as Paraguay. I'd still have to pay. Who's going to bat your sheets out every evening? You? Sleep with scorpions. Be my guest. Ah." The coolness and the slowness. The stem of a glass, held. "You already are."

New father ignored the purpose of this reminder, which he does until he can't, and then it is like the old scenes, when Papa used to rub Mum's head with the awful jam.

Konrad—"I agree it's vulgar. It isn't art. We shouldn't have such hierarchies."

Mum—"Oh, really? Then how do you account for what Baldomero's paintings are fetching, versus, say, your own?"

This was very cruel of her, because Konrad despises everything about Baldomero Zayas, except his giant art.

"Maybe just someone to do the cleaning, then," C. offered. "Konrad's a good cook."

Mum—"Yes, why not do away with them?!" (She had trouble pushing her chair out.) "I'll finish dinner in my room!" And she shook the service bell.

~~Mañana~~ la matina?

If I have learned one thing about being a woman, it's that men will change your mind. This morning there aren't any servants in white dresses and there isn't anything to eat. There are a lot of instruments out on the table to potentially make breakfast with, but everyone comes into the kitchen and stares at them, and knows not what to do, so the artists are walking around with bright glasses of red tea the cook left out to cool, but even that's all gone now, and everyone's confused.

Mother is lying in her green robe, enjoying the sun. Quite pleased with herself, she won't even tell the others where she's sent them. If I know mother, last night Konrad got to her. *Lea, je t'en prie.* Or maybe he found it in him to hold her: she'd send the staff to kingdom come, for that.

In any case, it could take eons to discern which of these pots holds the salt and which the sugar, and so the loons walk around listlessly, muttering to one another, admiring the flowers that I've never been able to name. Magda used to tell me the names of them, in Spanish, but I haven't retained anything, because I'm constantly being put into situations where I have to learn new things.

C. woke, though, and she is prone to hangovers. She closed her eyes when she saw the waiting kitchen, and opened them, and worked. By that evening, we had coffee. I exaggerate, but you have to boil all the water here because of what's inside it, and you have to light a fire to boil things. It is not unlike living in a coal bunker, Costalegre without staff.

Artists I like here:

FERDINAND CHEVAL

First of all, I love his name which reminds me of the bull
who preferred smelling the flowers to those awful bull-
fights. He is aptly named, as Ferdinand is the calmest,
nicest person here. He's a professional rock collector. He's
also a postman. Legrand even made him bring along his
uniform, which he wore over on the plane ride, and
proudly, I should say.

Mum told me that many years ago, Ferdinand started
collecting rocks during his rounds. I guess he's been mute
forever, so postman is a good job for him. He communi-
cates without talking. He bears news without his mouth.

He's got this lovely, weepy mustache, but he's actually
quite handsome, with high cheeks and burning eyes and
very clear, bright skin.

Konrad is fond of him, and most terribly protective.
Although he looks young and intelligent, Ferdinand is one
of the oldest artists here. Konrad said he's been collecting
rocks and seashells for over thirty years. That he started

off by putting them in his mail satchel but found so many
beautiful ones, he had to push around a wheelbarrow; that
he was quite the sight in town. That the people he deliv-
ered the mail to would greet him with odd rocks.

Ferdinand Cheval ended up building a whole palace
with his rocks. My brother has been to see it, and when we
were younger, and he hadn't found that stupid school yet,
he would sit on the end of my bed and tell me the most
fantastic tales. Apparently, it is a real castle, although it
looks melted, with oyster-shell corridors and spires topped
with pineapples and bended gray stairwells.

The whole of it has a plaque outside it and my brother
loved the words. "In building this rock, I wanted to prove
what will could accomplish." My brother told me that
after people visit it, they sit down and weep, so moved
are they that Ferdinand didn't have to build it, but built
it anyway.

My mother took a pilgrimage to see it along with Legrand
and Konrad, and of course she chose to go when it was my
time to be with Papa and Steph's time to be with her. In any
case, Legrand decided Ferdinand was a surrealist hero and
he made all the other artists go down south to see it.

As I said, Konrad was very taken by this silent man.
One of my favorite paintings by new father is of a winged
postman crawling toward a chimney of a house that is
slipping into a sea populated by mermaids and a pert

white whale. It's one of Konrad's paintings that look sort of real when you step back from them—in this one, the gate in front of the house is an actual gate that is attached to the picture's frame, and there is a real buzzer made of rubber near the door of the dream house for the postman to ring.

Unfortunately, Ferdinand suffered an emotional collapse because in order to finish the rock palace, he'd started working through the night. Legrand brought him to a sanatorium in Switzerland, but he missed his rounds.

I don't know how they got Ferdinand to come to Mexico. He doesn't seem unhappy. In any case, by the time we left Paris, they had stopped the mail.

WALTER FRITZ

Walter is big and nice and German, with a tall flop of white hair, and he can draw anything in the whole world. Walter was one of the most important artists to get out because he did all our exit papers. Not mine or Mum's, of course, as we're American, but you should see Ferdinand's. His look realer than our real ones!

Walter used to come round the Paris house and draw pictures of the parties that Mum throws. He'd do her with her huge honk of a nose and she wouldn't even care because he gave her such good eyes and a great figure, which is all she cares about. She keeps the one he did of her in her favorite cloth-of-gold dress and the shiny headpiece in her room.

When we're at long dinners, Walter will slip me a cartoon to make me laugh. Sometimes he'll put it in the bread basket and say, "Lara, are you sure you don't want more bread?" Usually, the drawing is of something funny happening at the table: Legrand red with anger, his open mouth filled with ducks.

There wasn't any of this fun on the way over. Walter's worried they'll come after him, the German customs agents, but mother says the Germans are too industrious to waste ten days on a boat.

BALDOMERO ZAYAS

I realize I'm still in the section of the artists that I'm fond of, but I can see Baldomero from the terrace where I'm writing; he's painting on the flat roof of his tower so that everyone can see him paint. So I shall write about him now. Baldomero is the most pompous person I have ever known, and given our (eternal?) company, that is really saying something. He goes everywhere with a perfectly turned-up mustache—he actually has someone who does it for him, and his mustache man would be here too except that Walter refused to make a passport for him and Mumma wouldn't pay.

Also, he wears a cape—a velvet one!—even though he's sweating. He has the strongest odor, and the oil he uses on his mustache smells of the pine oil that Grandmum used to coat the furniture with every time that we had guests.

He's absolutely despicable and he only eats shellfish. Normally there's always a separate plate for him, so I guess he'll either starve or learn how to get down to the beach himself. Or maybe he's got all the staff with him in that tower, I don't know, and I'll never know, because I'm only too glad not to have to go anywhere near it.

Everyone hates him. I don't even think that they're jealous of him; he's too famous and he does work rather hard. I suppose he thinks he's outlandish with his odd tastes and his posturing, but when it's every day like that, it's just tiresome for the house. I think if there's one person the Germans should have imprisoned, it is Baldomero. He does these paintings of unmentionables: men's parts and the women's, large and growing and covered in pink sand. Real Papa is a great hater of his paintings; he covered them with linens where they were stacked up in the hallway and would sigh each time Mum brought home another canvas. "Just another picture of a man cleaning out his rifle," he'd say, to make her frown.

I am not supposed to understand, of course, but I'm not blind to the pictures, and even if there weren't pictures, I have other people's words.

I've heard Hetty gossip that this is why Baldomero always gets a separate place to live, because of the weird touching, but I also think it's because he smells so much.

In any case, Mum is fond of mentioning how many Baldomeros she has in her collection and how very much they're worth. I guess he is her hostage, in a certain sense.

C.

Sometimes I want hair like hers, so fluffy and dark, it kind of floats around her face like an evil halo. I love that in the evenings, she paints her lips with red, but the rest of the day she stomps around looking like a peasant. C. writes all day, every day. She takes only two breaks for a quick walk, and she never stops for lunch, although she always stops for cocktails—that's when she ends her day. Or that's not true, exactly, because at some point, she'll ride the horses they have here. I just don't know when yet. I guess at her place in England, she has horses at the house. I don't think she sleeps a great deal, and she drinks like all the rest of them, but her voice is always nicely toned and she is levelheaded, with a good sense of humor, which is why Mum is fond of her, despite herself.

Undecided:

CASPAR DIX

Caspar is the photographer from France, the one who got the soup on his nice shirt. I guess Caspar was in trouble too because he took photos of the "degenerates" back home and sometimes in the nude. I'm not sure if it was only Baldomero who brought him or if Mum helped, but someone is lording over him; he has that sludge about him. You know the people who are resentful, even if they get to be in a nice place. Probably he thinks that this work is beneath him, trying to get a portrait of Baldomero with a wild monkey. In any case, I heard him complaining in French to Mum about how he'll never be able to develop anything because Mexico's too bright.

KONRAD BECK

He'd be so beautiful if he were happy. Sometimes at the parties when I catch the way he is with C., I hate my mother for the way she has to have the things that everybody likes. They weren't that awful together, before they were married. There was a time, actually, when Konrad was nearly affectionate with her!

But she had to win, as always. She still buys his art!

That's how much he loathes her: nothing is ever free. When we go out to restaurants, just the three of us, she asks him to pay the bill, and makes the waiter wait while he closes his eyes because he knows exactly what is coming, mother making quite the show of saying, "Oh? You still don't have any money? I'll pay."

Konrad does paintings like Baldomero's, except they never make you want to laugh and they're much harder to discern. I've been in some of his pictures. We both have. I was painted as an angel. Mum had the head of a horse.

Loathe!:

HETTY COLEMAN!

You know that Hetty cried today about the water? Said if she had to spend a full hour waiting for the water to boil, how in the world was she ever going to have time to write? And that she can't work without her tea. I'm not convinced that Hetty has ever written a single word of her great novel. But she certainly speaks a lot about the things that are keeping her from writing it.

I will say one nice thing, and that's that I like her figure. It's very charming and welcoming, if she weren't just so awful! What I mean by this is that she has a delightful bosom. Mumma has no chest at all, and C.'s is far too large. Hetty is the kind of woman you would want to be held by, if you could.

ANTOINE LEGRAND

Is the Father of Surrealism, and also a communist, although a bad one because he pushes his ideas on other people and never listens to theirs. He lived with us in Paris while he was publishing his manifesto on surrealism, which he has already changed a hundred times. Legrand makes useless objects and then he calls them art. He hammered a bunch of nails into Mum's electric iron, the part that's supposed to do the clothes. And although it's kind of funny, it isn't as if Legrand doesn't like nice things too. Also, he ruined Mum's iron and the maid got shocked.

Like the entire lot of them except for my own mother, Legrand doesn't have any children and I don't know if he cares for anyone in the way that makes it difficult to think of anyone else. Mostly, I think he needs my mother because she finds him fascinating, tells everyone he is.

Legrand owns nearly as many Baldomeros as Mumma and is constantly asking her to sell him the one of the elephants on circus legs that he told her to buy.

Stupid stupid Antoine Le-Grandest is everywhere around. He got Mumma into all the artists. She wanted to be a nurse before she met Antoine Legrand!

<u>What I wish for my own paintings:</u>

I would like for my art to be freer than it is now. I always feel like I am coloring inside the most childish lines. And even though the artists compliment my shading, it feels like a trick sometimes, how my artwork is realistic. You just don't get the kind of feeling from my paintings that you do from Konrad's. His work is probably the best if you take all the different aspects into consideration, the things he doesn't boast about. Even with Baldomero, even though it is technically perfect, you don't get that feeling that I long so badly for. As if something is intensely private, but also clearly seen.

Sometimes I think I am horrible and worthless. But then other times, I will really <u>feel</u> that thing inside, and everything falls back and it is as if I'm in the middle of a giant shell. I have been told that I have talent—Magda used to save my paintings and real Papa loved my colors. But no one says I have a gift.

Sometimes what I really feel is that I am burning up inside to have someone just for me, and that is what I am trying to get onto the canvas. Because that one time I had

Elisabeth back when I was in school for just that while, that's the feeling I had—the same feeling, that this was the right place, the only place that matters.

But Mumma will keep on moving if I can't make something beautiful. That's what I want. To make something truly beautiful. To make something that stays with you in that upsetting way.

She is ~~elegant~~ <u>beautiful</u>

She is <u>slender</u>

She ~~is~~ <u>isn't</u> <u>here</u>

Miércoles

So it turns out that Ferdinand knows how to make coffee, and he even served us eggs. Baldomero wants the staff back because he found a scorpion in his room. There are small brooms by the beds for this purpose and you need to keep on shoes.

C. has already started up her schedule. I see her in the morning and then she locks herself away all day. I have seen her room and it has the most attractive desk that looks right over the ocean. I looked in during one of her walks around the property. She had a giant stone on all her papers so they wouldn't blow away.

Viernes

The funny thing about the artists is they all look silly naked. Except for new father, who looks quite grand with height, and Mum, I suppose, who really is quite charming in her bathing suit. But C. goes in naked, and it's an awful lot. There is just so much of her, is what I mean. Legrand is pudgy, like a little bear, and Baldomero is too "furnished" to ever go near water.

The odd thing about my mother, though. She loves life around the pool. What a time we had in California when she bought me that large hat! She loves to have a drink with ice in it and stretch out her long legs, which truly are so lovely. She is probably at her best when she is lounging in this way. The pool water doesn't bother her, even if it's deep. We can all go swimming. Not that anyone here really knows how to swim, except for C. of course, who knows everything. But Mum didn't tell the new ones that they can't go in the sea. Caspar didn't know about the banishment and he got his head handed back to him this morning when he came home from Teopa with wet hair. Mum assumes that everybody knows in the way she assumes everybody knows everything she thinks. Poor Grandpapa went down on the Republic, so no one is allowed to swim inside the ocean. Even though she's constantly boating on it or letting horses near it, her guests cannot swim. The ocean is a place that takes you. That is how it is.

So naturally Caspar is even more upset than before. Plus he can't find a darkroom. He was setting up one of the maids' rooms as a darkroom but now Mum says perhaps she'll bring them back because she thinks it's disheartening to sort out your own lunch. I don't think Caspar speaks Spanish so I don't know where he'd go, and Mum certainly isn't going to pay for him to leave. The only town is Zapata and it's really not that close. You couldn't take a normal automobile there even if you had one; the road is full of holes and cows. There's just a place to get tortillas and another where they'll snap a chicken's neck right there when you buy one, so aside from the funny children and the donkeys for his photographs, what would Caspar do? I guess he would take pictures. But the closest biggest town is Guadalajara and that's days and days away.

Mum will have to go out soon if she doesn't get the staff back, because everyone wants news about the art boat and the Führer. There are almost five hundred paintings on the ship, mostly Mum's collection but some of Legrand's too, and supplies that Baldomero and some of the other artists need. Mother is in a terrible state because Hetty says the boat could sink, and she keeps bringing it up when there is nothing else to talk about: Do you think that it could sink?

Another thing that no one has considered is how we are to post letters. Even if the staff was back to go in and out of town for us, how could something get from here to Stephan? It could take years with all the chaos, and by that time Stephan will have graduated and we'll all be living somewhere together, probably stupid France. I'm still going to try, though. I'm still going to write him. He asked me to, you know.

One other thing that's funny: Mumma had to fill the shipping crates in the big boat with household things from Paris in order to qualify for moving. I don't know why but you can't ship only art. So Mum packed up our piano and some carpets and a couple of chandeliers, and then we ran around the house together trying to catch Legrand's gray cats even though I knew she wasn't going to send them; Mum doesn't really like cats but we had a laugh about them traveling across the ocean and how fat they are.

Of course, Baldomero is very eager to be photographed on the beach in his cape while playing the piano, but everyone else agrees that the best place for a grand piano is under the *palapa*, if they can get the piano up the hill to here. "The Rhineland's taken, and you talk of a piano," is what Caspar said to that. I actually think that he is Belgian, and not French.

Altercation

Hetty is worried that C. is putting things into her book that Hetty confessed to her in private. "I'll burn it if you snitched!"

Now C. goes for her daily walks with Ferdinand's mailbag, her manuscript rolled inside it. I imagine she sleeps with it underneath her pillow, the birds circling outside.

Altercation

Legrand played one of his stupid games last night. Everyone removed clothing until they felt uncomfortable. Of course, to prove who was the most surrealist, most of them ended up wearing nothing. New father was looking at C. with what Mum calls his "wet eyes."

"If you rise, the dollar will fall," she said.

Lunes

I've been down to see the horses. You know, we actually did a lot of riding when we were here last, because real Papa's very good. I like horses, as long as they're not too big, and don't have a suspicious air about them, and don't get those red nostrils. I would give anything to be like C., who can get on one from the ground, and who rides in her navy skirt. She looks so brave with her dark hair and her snug beige jacket, her hair touching her shoulders just so!

Mum calls it a hothouse, but I quite like the stables here, the big sky and all the fronds. There's a polo field across the way that's gone yellow from the drought, but I can hear the grooms shouting from my bedroom, *"Abierto, abierto!"* The horses have to be kept in good physical condition in case the owners visit, so they play on despite it. Hetty, who is an animal lover, says that it's a death sentence to play in such a heat, and that she is going to speak to the horses' minders. "In what language?" C. teased her. "Body?" And Hetty turned bright red.

The stables aren't like proper stables, not like in France or England. They're not really stables at all, just bright cuts of fabric strung up in the trees, and ropes to mark the horses' feeding places. At night, when they have the torches going and the stars are out, the shelters look like glowing kites. It's romantic and gay, and what with the grooms always singing and joking in their Spanish, it's really something fine.

I must get the courage to go riding alone lest I die of boredom. It wouldn't be right for me to go with Konrad and C.; it would be like we're a family, and we're not. Mother can't go anymore because of her poor ankles. I worry all the time that they will be coming for me too, but I've been doing the strength exercise on the steps just like the doctor told me: you stand on the edge of the step on tiptoe, and raise your body up and down using just the energy in your toes. It's difficult and painful but it will keep my circulation healthy and my bones won't deteriorate the way that Mum's are doing.

Domingo

I find myself thinking a lot about my dear Elisabeth. What else am I to do? Of course, I think a lot about my brother, also, but I know what he is doing, so it isn't as much fun. As for Elisabeth, I don't even know what country she's in; maybe she's still in Hertfordshire, where it was so nice. Our house there was lovely, even in the damp, and there was almost always a sturdy fire going. Papa walked me to school, you know, and all the buildings were made of the roundest funny stones, and at the end of the day, Lisabeth would walk back with me, and Doris would give us steak and kidney pies, and then we'd go outside and throw sticks for the doggies, and Stephan would flirt with both of us a little, and we'd run up the rocks.

That was the last school I was in, really, and that's when I was twelve. Mother's great collection takes her all sorts of places, so it takes me places too. In the years since the stone house, I have lived in four places in England and five places in France, plus one winter each in two different parts of Spain. Plus, there was the autumn we were in New York City when Mum was trying to start a gallery with the Metropolitan Museum, but that didn't work because Mum said she doesn't sleep well in New York, while she sleeps very well in Paris. So we went back. This was a mistake because the French don't even like her. Or not the ones in charge. Do you know, she went and offered her collection to the Louvre? Or rather, asked them to house it if there was war, and if there <u>was</u> war, that she would leave them with some paintings at the war's end? I saw the letter from the director, because Mum was so upset by it. Or rather, not upset, she was sort of off her head about it. She had Legrand paint some of the choicest lines on canvas and nail them around the house and then she had a party to celebrate what a foolish person the museum director was. "You will soon find you are propagating mediocrity; if not thrash . . ."

"Can't even spell trash!" Mum went around singing. "Too good to spell trash!" And so we went on a mad tour around Europe stashing this and that in barns, but then Legrand got in her head about the mice and rotting so we went on another tour to get all the paintings and the sculptures back. Then Mum put them on the big boat along with our piano, and most of the degenerates responsible for that art. It's true it really would be something if the boat should sink. Mother laughs sometimes and says if war comes and the boat gets shot, I should fix my sights on a woman with a solid fortune, because women are loyal and not hysterical with money, and they don't get called to war. Neither Papa nor Stephan will be called to fight, that's the good thing about having a Swiss passport. Not that they'd want Papa anyway. He's terribly lethargic.

Anyway, I am probably never going to get married and I'll either have a lot of children, or else I will have none. Maybe I <u>will</u> get married, though, and show my family a lovely, pretty time like we had in England. In any case (I don't feel that I should write this!), I'm still a *demoiselle*!(!) Elisabeth got hers when we were leaving Hertfordshire. She pinned a rag into her undergarment and the pin popped through and stuck her during Mrs. Ruthlace's cursive class. Her older sister brought her a mooncup back from London, which really made us laugh. Actually, "mooncup" is a good name for the stables, because all of those bright triangles look like they're trying to catch something from the moon.

I bet I never get it. Mum said she never did. A miracle, she said, both me and Stephan, making it to life. Mum always says it's nice to eat only a little so that you feel poetic, and I try to do this, but it makes me feel sad and it's hard to get my words in the right order. I'm just silly when I'm hungry, silly to be around, is what I mean. And

Elisabeth says you never get your monthlies if you don't eat, that she got hers because she was always finishing my steak and kidney pie.

I go back and forth on it. Sometimes it's true when I'm hungry I do get that poetic light feeling, and think I'd like to be married very much. But other times when I have my wits about me, I remember Papa making Mum lie down on the carpet so he could march across her belly when he'd had a horrid writing day. And Konrad and Mum have such a storm about them. But then I see the way he is with C. and I think how nice it would be to have someone to hold you and to tell all your secrets to, instead of you, small diary, who has no arms at all.

Some words for my mother:

headboard
the wires here for bats
the swimming area at the beach pond cordoned off with
   buoys
pink melon frappé
the ghost town of Pampino stories (which probably doesn't
   exist)
awful marzipan
"the buying of the rains now"
a purple made from shellfish
her white long legs are my legs
lemon water (warm)
"How I despise myself"
the pink hole in her pillow
the painting of the gazelle
heavy leaves in England
the fire going out
also, lemon pulp (and bitters?)
her foot in ankle cast
the scorpion in orchid
¿
¿

the largest, biggest hat

One day, though, with the memories. All the flashes in one place. The time she took me out of school because she wanted to go driving and we drove up the English seaside looking for some ice cream, and we had the windows open and the ocean waves were fin-colored and the ice cream parlor was closed, and we walked to the cliff even in the wind there and she held me to her in the freezing, "Oh! My gorgeous girl!"

Miércoles?

It is almost dinner and I never did get lunch. Ferdinand went rock hunting and C. has her door shut and none of the artists know what to do with the strange things in the larders. Half the people here have never seen such fruit before, and in any case, most of the artists have made off with the oddest ones to paint them or smash them and draw things with their juice. There are already four pineapples and a dining chair floating in the pool.

I tried to find mother to ask if she couldn't bring back the cook, as she said she might, and perhaps also the maid, but she is always talking fervently with Legrand in her green raincoat or standing at the bottom of the dirt driveway, waiting for news about her boat.

<u>Some things for my brother:</u>

If I had been born first, he would have been the same brother, still clever and impatient, but light enough to carry, like something I could steal. I remember when we walked our two dogs into the forest, how he was the one who picked up a green pinecone and then another pinecone and he put them at the opening of the second biggest tree and he said, "When those open, that will mean that we can go into the tree," and I said, "What will we do there, won't it be dark?" and other things that shame me now because my questions were so usual, and he said, "We'll be safe," and because he was older, I said, "Safe from what?" and then my dog, who was always the frightened one, started barking at the tree.

Viernes

The staff is back. No one knows their proper names so Mum calls the men "Eduardito" and the women "Rosa." Mum says she sent them all back to Zapata for a couple of days; she told them to make it back for Friday, serves the artists right.

Hetty has a small book of Spanish phrases in case of an emergency. I asked her if I could see it, and I practiced most of the morning, and then I waited until everyone was outside of the house or working to use my sentence with the cook. "*¿Dónde está Magda?*"

"*Pobrecita!*" the cook said, and then she pulled out a wooden stool for me and had me sit and touched my back and cut up a papaya. It is really something thrilling, all of those dark seeds. She put them on a piece of parchment paper and spoke to me in Spanish, gesturing with her hands. She acted out what she wanted: she wanted me to go outside and dig and plant them, to make a papaya plant.

I don't know why but the idea of doing this made me want to cry. The idea of digging by myself, I guess, or whether or not I'd ever see what grew.

"*Pobrecita*," she said again, rubbing my back and the hair she says is gold.

It's only as I'm writing this that I realize she never told me where Magda went to, so maybe I didn't say the sentence right.

Lunes

Jose Luis has been to town and he has news about the Führer. Hetty has let me borrow her Spanish phrase book as long as I don't spill on it or drop it in the pool or in some other water, and it has to be back in her room each night in case one of the Mexicans tries to compromise her, she says. Regardless, I learned that the cook is named Maria and the houseman, Jose Luis. He goes to town on one of the ponies in the barn and comes back with flour and sugar and strange vegetables in the saddle sacks.

Jose Luis has a porter friend in Puerto Vallarta who helps people with their luggage, and he says that the country of Japan has invaded China, according to one of the white men getting off a boat. "What was the nature of his business?" Walter wanted to know about the man in question, but Jose Luis couldn't say.

There was much speculation then of what this meant and of where Japan and China were in respect to us in Mexico, and once a decision was reached, Hetty wanted to know if this meant that the waves would get even bigger at Teopa, but Baldomero refused to translate for her, saying that she was one of these people whose brain was an insult to her head. The only reason he agreed to talk to Jose Luis in the first place was to have news of the boat, but Jose Luis says that all the other white men are asking for news of the Führer, so that is what he brought back from Zapata, and Baldomero called him a silly man, and said next time to ask for detailed information about their boat, because that boat carried the future of art history and most of Jose Luis's pay.

Lunes

For dinner all the girls were back in their embroidered dresses and we had fish on thick white plates. Baldomero had something you had to tug out of a seashell and mother wore her cloth-of-gold dress and all was right and lovely. Hetty had a stomachache and spent most of the meal silent, which made C. relax and be more generous than we're used to. "But Hetty!" she said. "You're such marvelous company when you're ill!"

Mother had that lovely glow about her that she gets when she has spent time with Konrad, and Konrad was beautifully dressed and in a dashing mood. You see! He doesn't always hate her. Most of the time, she is complimentary about his work, and she didn't even mind the one where she has a horse head, because it was a startling painting and he's fond of horses, he's always said how much. She can be funny and quite clever, my little Mumma-Mum. Konrad can forget that because she spends so much time picking out dressing items and fussing with her mouth, but she's really very witty, and when he remembers that, and sees other people admire her, we have the perfect nights. How lovely for it that we got one of those nights, now.

The news of Japan invading China has brightened everyone. No one knows anybody over there and only Legrand and Baldomero have been: they both agree that nothing matters unless the Japanese take Bali, which is a spiritual place where, they said, the castles look like Ferdinand's rock castle in France. That is why Ferdinand is such a totem to them: he is able to go places mentally where he's never even been.

There was also talk about a man named Jack. I don't know him, but mother says I do, that I met him here last time. I wanted to argue that I would have remembered meeting a new person, but she was speaking kindly, and, in any case, I didn't want to stick up for myself because the artists make loud noises when I blush.

Apparently Jack came in the 1920s, when all the art was in Vienna and Mumma met the Hollywood film man who told her about the place in Costalegre that he'd built. Mumma bought a house, she laughed, did they all remember that, she bought that pink casita without ever seeing it, over that odd beer. And she brought all of her friends with her to see the home she'd bought, and one of them was

Jack. "Mr. Da-da-da," Legrand hooted, and I will tell you that the way he laughed about it made me think that Legrand hadn't been included in that trip.

Well, Jack came back to Mexico after the stock crash. The Viennese were writing out their grocery lists on banknotes, which seems awfully vulgar, so I don't know if it was just the artists doing this or the regular people also, but the point was that Jack bought a house from the Hollywood man as well. This got everybody laughing, I guess about Jack's house. "I will say that Mr. Hollywood saved the worst houses for the *messieurs!*" is what Legrand added, but I bet you, I just bet you, that it's a perfectly fine house.

I don't know how much time Jack spent here before that, but C. said that when the Führer put an end to modern painting, Jack moved to Costalegre permanently. "And stopped painting!" Legrand announced, a little happily, I'll note. That was almost four years ago and no one has seen him since.

"We should send Eduardo out to see if he's still here," Mum said.

(I've told her his name is Jose Luis but she doesn't mind it. She says it's more romantic, Eduardito, and that he thinks so too.)

"He was so talented," Mum said.

"Intolerable," Legrand.

"He probably wouldn't even want to see us," said mother. "He didn't care for us much, at the end."

"You see," said C., winking, "he really is a clever man."

After that, I went up to bed to avoid another of their games, and also because I wanted to sleep with the idea that the evening had been pleasant. In the game they've played most lately, they force each other to look at someone else and then say something true. The idea is to do this with no clothing, so it will be true. I'm always worried one will stray and come up naked after on the stairs. Hetty's always worried about the lovely Mexicans, while I'm worried about <u>them</u>. I asked Mum to build me a real door and she said that she'd ask Walter, but I don't think she has.

My room is the most gorgeous place at night, even better than the stables because there aren't so many flies. You look out and except for the moon and whatever's reflecting in the ocean, it's dark as dark can be. Sometimes I swear I can see the reflection of the moon in the slipping whales who slide in and out of the water that I'm never going to get to go into. Perhaps it's just as well. Think of all the things that you're sharing the sea with, and not only the whales. Mumma, when I was little, would tell me how Grandpapa dressed for dinner when he knew the ship was going down. How he put his mistress on a lifeboat and got on his tuxedo, or actually, he probably put the tuxedo on first because it was the mistress and some of the other survivors who said that there had been men awaiting death in style on the upper deck, and that one of them had been my grandfather. Mum has always been so proud of that, the fact that he went down in such a brave and elegant fashion. When I think of swimming underwater, I think of swimming through the shattered wineglasses and the twisting, slow cravats.

Day?

It is funny, when you have time for the remembering. I'm thinking of those dogs. Stephan's was Sir Herbert. I don't remember what I wanted mine to be; we'd been given them by neighbors. They were puppies, but it seemed like only a week that they were small, a week that was full of presents and much time spent in the house.

Mumma wanted me to name mine after her. "Go on and call it Leonora!" she told me, calling after it, trying to get my little dog to come.

Jueves

There is a new crisis. Hetty has started to go on walks with me to the stables and there is a situation with a goat. There is a small goat tied to one of the partitions where the horses stay. He's got a clever air about him. But when you see only one goat, it's always a bad sign. Hetty's in a state about it; the fragility of animals causes her such pain. The goat is going to be killed, she says, and probably right there. We went back there with our phrase book: "*¿A qui questa cabra?*" I don't think we got it right, but after much back-and-forth and hand signing, the groom said it was Señor Jack's.

Hetty became red as she always does. "You tell the *señor* there'll be no goats killed today!" And then she went to take the goat, and the man became very angry. Hetty told him she would see about this situation with Señor Jack himself, and she picked her way around the horse manure and untied the goat herself. The man protested greatly, but in Spanish, so Hetty said we had no choice but to leave his protests behind. It took us two hours to get the goat up to Occidente; he didn't want to go. He kept standing stiff in place and bleating, no matter how we tugged the rope.

Once we got him up to the house, Hetty realized she didn't know what goats eat, so she tied his rope close enough so that he could get to the garden, and we went in to get him a bowl of water, and when we came back, he'd knocked most of the lemons off a lemon tree. But there was shade and the grass that is so thick here, so he seemed all right.

Hetty marched back into the house and called, "No one touch that goat!" Maria left the kitchen to see what Hetty was yelling about, and she got that expression she gets when anybody here talks to her, halfway between sadness and making fun of what was said.

Hetty said she was going upstairs to write a letter to Jack about why he was killing helpless animals, and have Eduardito deliver it straightaway, and how was she ever going to work on what she was supposed to be working on, when she had to take care of <u>this</u>? Didn't anyone care about the emotional well-being of the animals and so forth. But she must have fallen asleep or started working on her novel because she was gone a long time. Legrand and Mum had started their cocktails round the pool when I went down to check the goat. And he was gone. His rope was too, which made me even sadder, picturing him trotting through the jungle with that blue rope trailing from his neck. The jungle is a horrid place with ticks and many burrs, and I knew it would get stuck on something, and that he would be frightened.

I knocked on Hetty's door and she was, in fact, asleep. I told her that the goat had disappeared, along with the blue rope. She was furious, and said that if the rope was gone, then surely one of the Mexicans had marched him right back down to the butchers, and how was she going to get any work done when she had to be saving animals' lives.

She told me to put on riding boots and half chaps against the thorns; we'd take a lantern, we would find him.

Well, we didn't need a lantern and we didn't need to go far. Beyond the lovely plantings there is a steep slope covered with all manner of pointy scrubs and furious cacti. The goat was about a ten-minute walk through this with his throat open. His blue rope snarled around a scrub of plants. The flies not even there yet.

"Oh," Hetty said, her mouth open. "Oh no."

I didn't cry until later, because I was so mad. Only a few hours before, the goat was happy with the horses, and then he'd had his throat gnashed by some horrid animal. Hetty said we had to run back because the animal was surely still around, probably a Bengal tiger, something just horrific, and I did get tears in my eyes then and we held our skirts up around the corners, and all the stupid stones. It was her fault that the helpless animal was ruined and he must have been so scared by whatever took him there.

When we got back, we brushed ourselves off outside the house, and Hetty reminded me that this was so unfortunate but not worth upsetting the others with the gruesome nature of the news; we would say the goat had escaped. And what a shame about it.

Then she pulled me to her chest, quite pleased about our pact. This made me feel good until Hetty went into the house and I remembered that no one knows what to do with all the kind things in the world.

Dear Stephan,

Things are terribly different at this house than they were at the casita, and it's a shame that you're not here. We've got everything in good working order, and the artists are advancing on their projects every day. I have designs to start riding a lot, but I haven't been able to because of the rain but also because I am painting quite a bit! I have had to switch from oil to gouache because we're almost out of oil paint—this isn't a bad development as the oil took forever to dry in the hot air.

Has the war arrived yet? This is silly of course, but you're so high up in the Alps there, I sometimes daydream about you seeing it, the way that you can see rain coming when you're low on the flat ground. I wonder if you'll hear it, and what you'll see. We're not getting much news here, and none about the boat, which has mother frantic even though she's trying not to be. As you know, the situation isn't helped by Hetty Coleman, who thinks very negatively and is convinced the boat will sink. I don't know why she's so worried about it; it isn't as if she owns any of the art inside it.

All right, so maybe I'm exaggerating a little bit, things aren't so organized at all. In fact, you remember how Papa had recommended a tutor, that nice Swiss girl from Bern? Well mother forgot to secure her exit papers, and so I'm stuck out here in the jungle without any schooling. I wasn't lying about the painting, though, or even about the horses. It's just hard to accomplish the ideas I have because of this great heat.

Oh and Hetty is an animal thief now; she stole somebody's goat and it escaped from Occidente and got its throat opened by some tiger. I really wish you were with us instead of in that stupid school. Never mind, I know. You'll become something terribly exciting and I'll come and live with you forever. Please do marry someone nice enough that I'll feel she's like a sister. I feel this way about C., but of course I can't <u>really</u> talk to her, and I'm not supposed to say anything flattering about her, as you well know!

I do hope for war sometimes, so that you'll have to flee. There can be accidents, you know, even over Switzerland. All sorts of things can now be dropped out of the sky!

How stupid that I don't have something interesting to tell him; all I do is complain. I can't even write something cultured about the landscape because I don't know their stupid names. Hetty has books on this, on fauna. I know she does because she carted a whole trunk of research items for her novel in the plane. I'll have to have a look-see when she goes down for her drinks.

Oh! And the hairless dogs he was so excited about last time, to say that they're not here. And that Caspar took a photograph of mother with a cherry over each of her closed eyes. Is he good at math, still? To send us a Swiss paper. And also, the stories Papa told us about the ropes they used to string up in the village to keep people from blowing away during the bora winds. Is it true? Has he held the ropes yet? Has he felt the wind?

Spanish:

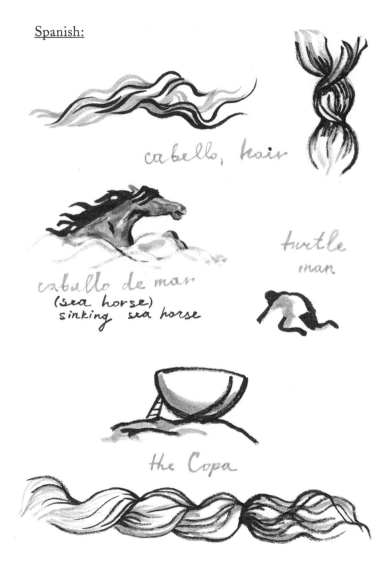

cabello, hair

caballo de mar
(sea horse)
sinking sea horse

turtle
man

the Copa

Among Hetty's books there was the nicest one called "Mexican Plants for American Gardens" by an intrepid little American named Cecile Hulse Matschat, who spent her time traveling around Mexico admiring pleasure gardens and writing everything down. She really seems to have the nicest way about her; perhaps she's English, actually, because she talks a lot about tea, and the nicest places to take it. But really, she has the nicest writing style.

Lotus-scented pools, cement rings for irrigation, red-tiled roofs, forgotten gardens on the outskirts of town—these are the notes I've been taking; don't they conjure up the most majestic world? She even describes the interior of buildings: "Broad, winning flights of stairs." What a lovely way to call a staircase! I wish that I could write as joyously as that! I quite like writing, but only for myself and in my letters. When I see what crafting something did to Papa, it doesn't make you want to share your private thoughts. But it's a wonderful feeling keeping all my thoughts right here. They're hidden, unlike paintings. Nobody can see them unless I want them to!

Chapters I shall read from Hetty's book:

A Patio in Guadalajara with Potted Plants, Brick
Benches, and Decorative Plaques   5

Tiled Fountain for Patio or Penthouse   38

Color with Bulbs!   8

Pink pepper
Jacaranda
Montezuma cypress
Mammillaria cacti?
Lantana
Wine-red morning glories
Vermillion bougainvillea
Ear flower?
Peaty bogs

And these are just the trees and plants and things I like
the sound of.

Hura
crepitans

Day?

The most terribly exciting thing has happened, diary. I have met Jack! I'd gone down to the stables to brush the horses and listen to the grooms sing, and there was a man and I knew it without knowing it that it was Jack.

He turned right when I arrived. He recognized me, I think! But first I want to describe the sensation of seeing him.

He didn't look familiar and yet I definitely knew him, so maybe it is possible that Mum's right (it's rarely) and I have met him before. It was like the air went yellow and I got a funny feeling in my stomach. I blushed right away, of course—I can never help it, no matter what I try. He was angry, also, he was in the middle of yelling in real Spanish, not <u>at</u> the groom, but with him. He had a letter in his hand. Of course I would put everything together later, but right then I was stuck on the fact that it was him and that he spoke such Spanish.

Anyway, Jack was wearing a loose shirt with faded stripes and proper jodhpurs. Also, a belt of the most cheerful yellow. Boots covered in muck. He was tall, maybe even as tall as Konrad, but it is difficult to say, really, because the horses here are smaller than they were in Europe and they make everyone look tall.

I've never been good at describing people, but I'd like to say "distinguished." You just felt right away that he was a very important man. He was wearing glasses and he had the whitest teeth. White and sharp like a line of something; how dull not to be able to properly explain it. I could paint it, though, a line coming through the dark. Thin lips and those lovely teeth that were almost child-like, I think.

He had a bird nose and a sharp chin, but these aggressions were lessened by his eyes, which were the softest shade of gray. I don't know how to describe this, but he had a daring smile. As if he had been walking around with a secret, and I was just the person to tell.

"Mademoiselle Lara?" he said, both he and the groom looking at me. And then he walked over; in fact, he was quite tall.

"But you're . . . you're a *princesa* now!" He turned and said something to the groom that made him laugh. "The last time I saw you, you were a real child," Jack added, done with whatever else he'd said before.

"Seven, eight," I said.

"And now you must be twenty!"

This made me laugh because of course I wasn't twenty; if I were twenty, I would be married and not down at the stables doing nothing by myself.

"I'm fifteen," I said. "Just."

He raised his eyebrows.

"Dangerous age," he teased. And I understood why many people must have liked, and also hated, him so much.

"Have you come to ride? Is your mother joining you?"

"Oh no," I said. "She can't with her ankles. They've gotten terribly worse. But we've got . . . Charlotte will ride. Do you know Charlotte?"

"Course I do," he said. "Terrific horsewoman. Fiendish writer. How many of you are up there at that hellhole?"

"Oh, I think we're . . . nine?"

"And which one of the imbeciles was it that stole my goat?"

I went even redder.

"Hmm," he said. "I see." Then he turned to the groom and said another thing in Spanish.

"It wasn't me, sir," I said quickly. "It was . . ."

"Tell away," he said, pulling the letter from his front pocket. "I know who, exactly. Hetty sent this over. What a perfect fool. Do you know that goat was payment for my friend, here?" he asked. "A little deal between gentle-men. And now that idiot Hetty has left me in debt to him."

"But," I said, kicking at the ground a little. "To kill?"

"Yes, of course to kill!" he answered. "What do you want them to eat, flowers? Is that what Hetty has you eating with that swarm?"

"I doubt she meant real harm."

"But of course she did," said Jack. "She's a meddler. She means harm before she causes it. That's what fools are for." He crammed the letter back into his pocket. "So how do I proceed? Shall I send Hetty out to find another goat for this good man?"

I heated even further thinking of what I knew, and that poor animal in the mountains, who was by now pecked to bits by the horrid vultures that are always hovering around.

"It would be better that she pay," I dared, "because if you bring another animal, she'll—"

"Her money's your mother's, and Leonora couldn't have had anything to do with this, she gets anemic without meat. How is she?" he asked, the twinkle in his eye not dulling, which made me feel happy for my Mum.

"She's well," I said. "Or rather—anxious—because she has no news of her boat."

"Is Hartnett down here, also? And your brother, his name, forgive me—"

"Stephan." I responded. "No, they stayed in Switzerland. They're not . . . my mother isn't married anymore. I mean, to him."

Jack covered his face with his hand. "Don't tell me. Don't." He took a breath, dramatically. "Do."

"She married Konrad. Konrad Beck? To get him out. Well, mostly."

"Oh dear God, of course she did. Always saving souls." He kept his mouth open to say something further, but he didn't say it. It was like he changed directions at the helm of a small boat.

"I'll tell you," he said, crouching a little to be with my same height. "You're fifteen. You should know. If you want to stay in love with someone, don't ever marry them. Konrad's a real artist. He's going to make your mother miserable."

"Yes, he's doing that, I think."

"Is he painting?"

"Trying to," I said, pleased that I'd been clever. "He was in an internment camp, before."

"Dear God."

"All of them are degenerates now," I blurted. "The Führer made a list."

"And he's right on that point, but that's the only thing I'll give him. I was kicked out myself, you know, but that was ages backward." He stood.

I hadn't had enough to eat and was less guarded with my talk than I might have been if I were full. Also, I knew enough to realize he'd soon mount and ride away.

"They're eager to see you, it sounds like," was what I came up with, so he'd stay. "They talked about you at a meal."

"Well, I hope it was a good one. Because if it was a bad meal, they were bored. A good meal, they were feeling good and thinking of me fondly." He pulled the letter out again. "So what am I to do?" He tapped the note against his pant leg. "You know it isn't easy to find a goat here, not in February. She's really put me in an awful place."

"He's dead," I blurted. "Hetty brought him up to the house and he escaped."

"Well of course he's dead. As if anything could survive a night up on that hellscape. It's amazing that you're here. Why are you? Shouldn't you be schooled?"

"We move too much. And Mum forgot a tutor."

"For the love of all that's . . ." he started. "What an awful mess. For God's sake, and who knows how long you'll be down here. You say she's waiting for a boat? War is going to come, you know. There's just no way around it. I respect your father but he's an idiot to have stayed. And for your brother to not be with you." He shook his head. "Leonora hasn't changed."

I blinked my eyes against all this information. But his words were also crumbs. It was exciting and also a little sickening to meet someone who had known my mother before I did. Probably Jack knew terrible things about her, like how she hadn't wanted children in the first place, and killed some after me. Of course no one is supposed to know that, but Mum can't keep a secret, not an important one like that. I think that she's too proud. And in any case, I was always in the house during her and Papa's fights.

"Well then, I'll have to come up to the hellhole." He looked skyward. "When?" he asked the sky. "Not tonight." He shook his head. "Tomorrow. Tell them I'd like to come at nineteen hundred hours, and that I want my goat. That'll put them in a state, the lot of them." He went to ruffle my head, and then, I don't know what. Realized how high my head was now.

He looked at me with his sharp, peculiar face. Like a great bird, but I don't know what kind of bird because I don't know anything!

"You look nothing like your mother," he said. "Or do you? It's so odd. There's something in the attitude but it might be more your dad."

When I look in the mirror, I don't think I look like either of them either, and it was disconcerting to see someone look as unsure as me. Papa's light and fair-skinned, and Mum is pale but freckled with her dark black hair, while I've got my hair and skin that tans if I'm not careful. My eyes are green, though. Like my mother's. That's one thing we have.

Jack did leave on a horse, you know. He already had one readied, and I guess he was taking it back to wherever it is he lives. He'd just come to see the man about the goat, but what nice timing for me.

Now I'll rush back to the house and tell Mum about the dinner. She does love parties and things to celebrate, so I'm sure that she'll be pleased. I have a few special dresses we brought over and won't it be exciting to welcome some-one new.

Domingo

Dinner was a real party, joyful and just bursting like they were before! Mumma even kissed me when I got to the palapa, and then she kissed Maria, who had helped me braid my hair.

Mumma went to all her efforts when she heard that Jack was coming. She laughed about the goat business and asked the cooks to cook some goat. Hetty was enlisted to make the place look festive, which mostly meant extracting the gnats from all the candles and the pineapples from the pool, but she did this without grumbling, my mother teasing her the whole time that she was sweet on Jack.

And I made a flan with Maria! It isn't difficult, actually: just sugar (when you sift, you watch for ants), eggs with yolks as orange as an orange, fresh milk and sweetest cream, and of course the milk here already smells like flan, sweet and grassy, like hay that's just been rained on.

There was a real shift in the group when they heard that Jack was coming. I discern that he's well-liked. Even

Caspar brightened, and Ferdinand made a pathway to the pool with the most charming stones.

Mumma thought it would be funny to cut shapes in all the napkins, but Legrand said that even with his Dadaism, Jack could be old-fashioned, that he liked collecting garbage but not ruining things. This was the first time I have ever heard Legrand be sensible, so he must like Jack too.

The biggest surprise was learning that Konrad and Jack are close. And C., also, they shared the longest embrace when he arrived wearing the same jodhpurs that I'd seen him in and a funny coat. In fact, Jack sat beside C. at the table and they were touching the whole time, like my mother and Legrand do when they're really into it, making sure the person's arm is there every time they make a phrase. They've had some life together, before I was born, the all of them. It makes me think that Mumma must have been delighted in Vienna. This was way before Mumma married anyone.

Of course, they spent most of the evening talking about art. If you were to listen to the artists here, you'd think there wasn't anything in the world but them. Except for Jack and C., and, I suppose, my mother, who likes to give everyone a chance, you'd be hard-pressed to hear a compliment out of Costalegre. Everyone and everything is "artificial" and "constrained." Well, it isn't true, you know. Out there in the French barns, my mother hid the strangest paintings. Collages with grim machinery bursting from human heads, violins that looked like corpses, naked female bodies separated into cubes. It gave you a sick feeling to look at them, seasick, almost. But I have learned from Mumma that the most important things are heralded by nerves.

The names of their belongings—cubism, Dadaism—it's meaningless unless you've seen it: the scavenged, rough materials, the serrated edges nestled into glue. When you've seen it, and when you hear the makers talk, you get a sense of what the movement is, but when you are away from it, it's like you have to memorize the same words that they've said, otherwise the meaning starts floating away, like when you are reading something wonderful but falling asleep at the same time.

"Have you seen any of Jack's paintings?" Hetty leaned toward me, during dinner. She was flushed and exalted through every course, none of which had goat. Jack has really stirred something up in them. Among them. They've always been mistrustful of the ones who work alone.

I said that I hadn't, and said nothing further so that I could hear the others. Konrad was in a rare mood and talking of Les Milles. This had mother nervous, because no one at the table had an idea how this would go. Konrad has to be very drunk or very proud to talk about the internment camp, and it rarely ends well. But this night, he had that shine about him, was sitting very straight. Wearing his great poncho, the red one with the yellow and blue stripes that my mother had had made for him; a pattern that matched up with his birth sign in the Chinese zodiac.

"Like here," he laughed, brandishing the fish speared on his fork, "only better food."

Everyone laughed. I laughed. Although it made me feel funny to laugh at something that wasn't.

"Many men of letters," Konrad continued. "Many lettered men. We had musicians too, and scientists. We could use a little of that here. Don't you all miss music?"

"Plenty of music," Jack said, "if you wake up with the grooms."

"I hear them from my bedroom!" C. added. "God, it's just divine."

"They scorn us, though. They do," went Konrad. "They think us spoiled fools. That we've never known a hardship." He darkened. "They have no idea."

Konrad looked down at the table and my chest went tight. I watched my mother swallow.

"Well!" said Mumma. "It's true you only have to go out on the balcony to hear their lovely songs. They drift up to us, it's charming, isn't it? Like . . . like . . ."

"Like songs," said Konrad, darkening after all.

"What I want to know," said Jack, in a light voice, "is what will become of our dear Lara." He gave a wink to me.

"And the proper answer, Lara, is engineer. An academic, if you must! Anything, anything, except one of our wrecks."

"She's quite good at painting," said C., smiling a smile she uses just at night. At the other end of the table, I felt my mother's lips close. "And a lovely little illustrator," C. continued. "So charming. And naive."

"Is that right?" Jack asked, because the table had gone quiet. "Good God, you don't want to be an artist, do you?"

"No, no," I answered quickly. "It's just a way of passing time."

Mother tented fingers over her big plate. "When we get through this war business," she said, "I'm going to organize a gallery show. Of child artists! Calaway *Jeune*," she giggled. "There's another boy, Lucian—his sketches, what a genius! You should see his faces, inscrutable, like charcoal lumps. But such a style about him. He's really quite inimitable, and at only twelve!"

That tightening in my chest again. How mother was incapable, or unwilling, to ever speak of me.

Most went back to eating, but Jack's face still held light.

"Intermission, I think, no? Lara, you partake?" he asked, holding up a pouch of what I assumed to be tobacco.

I blushed. "Oh, no, I'll just . . ."

"You know about the comb jellies?" Jack stood. And reached his hand out, all the way there at the table's end, and everybody watched. "Come."

I suppose the others realized they were making up for an insult and sat tightly, but what a miracle that my mother didn't rise. She can't stand to share her guests, especially the new ones. And usually, she doesn't recognize she's hurt me, so it couldn't have been that.

We walked out of the vast palapa, past the pool where Ferdinand had put a candle in between each of his small rocks. We walked to the corner where the main house started, the hot air like an exhale that wouldn't ever move. Jack was pinching tobacco into paper, intent on this one task, and he didn't embarrass me further by asking if I intended to smoke.

I felt very nervous. It wasn't clear if he would ask about my art or say something of my mother; both options felt equally horrifying at the time. I'm sure that C. meant "naive" as a compliment, because it is a word the loonies use; the highest praise, really, when art is childlike. But I am too young to be naive in an interesting manner. My paintings are naive because I'm not any good at it, or not good yet. I keep trying to have my work be loose and strange, but I gather that you have to be a draftsman before you can take everything apart.

"Comb jellies," Jack said, staring at the sea. "You see them? Glowing?"

It's always made me nervous, looking for something that someone already sees. It's like you have to find it quickly, lest they think you foolish, and there is that odd sensation while they are waiting for your eyes to capture what theirs have already seized.

The night was so warm, and the strange insects were all humming. But I saw the glow. Almost turquoise, off to the right in the black and moving waters. Then gone. Then there again; more pure blue this time.

"They're predators," Jack said, putting away his pouch. "Not too many know that. Huge, gigantic mouths." He crossed his arms with a shrug. "You know why it is they glow?"

I got that feeling that I always do, as if I'm going to cry. It is so rare that someone talks to only me!

"I don't know anything," I said.

"Well, that isn't true, now. You've made it all the way to Mexico with a ship of fools and you still have your head facing the right way. That isn't nothing, you know."

He took a draw of what he'd rolled.

"They light their tentacles up as decoys," he said. "When the prey comes, they cover their victims in a bioluminescent slime. They let them swim around like that, shining their whereabouts for everyone to see. No rush for them, really. When the glow starts to fade, they eat. Shows you what you get for following something beautiful." He shrugged again.

"Is it true that you don't paint anymore?" I shouldn't have spoken so quickly, but I had that pressured feeling again, as if he were going to leave.

"Is it true that you want to be an artist?"

I was able to look at him, this time. He was very tall against the darkness.

"I would like to be something good."

I watched him take a breath. He contemplated the whole of me. I even felt my toes pressing against the edge of my cloth shoes.

"Shall we go back?"

I never get to stay in conversations for as long as I would like.

Viernes

Many days have passed and the heat is intolerable and Jack has not come back. It should have rained by now, it should be pouring, but the rain doesn't come and the heat doesn't break and the trees are all there, waiting.

All the artists feel it, and no one is doing the right work. Even C. is raised shoulders and pinched mouth, stomping up and down the dirt driveway too many times a day, embarrassed that we're seeing her, that we see that she's not writing.

Only Hetty's working well, because of course she revels in others' misery, has to come out "on top." Mother is listless and wants another party; she's been walking round the house with her peacock scepter, sighing about the news.

Jose Luis came back from Zapata with the two telegrams mother had prepared: one for the shipping company and one for my father, neither of which were sent.

The man who runs the telegram went to Guadalajara and won't be back for a long time. My mother asked for specifics, how much of a long time, and Jose Luis said that no one there could say.

Hetty said the boat has surely sunk by now; it's been over three weeks. As for me, of course it would be ghastly if it <u>had</u> sunk, but I can't imagine Occidente holding more people than it does already. I hate sharing the bathroom. Even though he's nice enough, Ferdinand always takes a long time there, and Caspar leaves a menacing smell in every room he exits, like a carpet that won't dry.

I imagine my brother Stephan seeing soldiers from his mountain. I imagine father not seeing them because he's trying to write. I imagine father struggling over paper while the soldiers charge up the mountain and into the small house. I imagine swimming with my entire body as one gelatinous glow, like a sack I can't get out of, swimming and swimming among the predators, not knowing when I'll sink.

I started painting jellyfish. But what do I know of the real sea? Been in only to my ankles, never dared go out myself. It's a good thing that I'm pretty; what else is there to hold? In any case, Mum's proud of my "fetchingness"; there's no getting around that. I asked her to take me to Teopa today, to see if there were turtles, but she said she was in too much of a state about the telegrams. That she had to nap. Sometimes it feels that mother would sleep herself into a world away from me, if she could. That she would sleep into a place where I would be the one to wake her, stroke her cheek and call her pretty, fall down near her ear coil and whisper which dress I like best.

My dear, dear, dear Elisabeth,

It's funny to write someone when you don't know whether the letter will get to where they are, but I suppose I can practice here until I know if you're in England.

I have much to tell you, and much I'd like to ask! If only you were here with me, it would be so different. I know you've seen the sea already but here it's filled with whales. There are also crocodiles and flamingos that are white.

When you have a lot of time for thinking, you tend to think of the odd things. There are so many people here who are really excellent at something, it makes me long for the things I've never tried. For example, how do I know that I'm not a brilliant swimmer, as I've never been allowed? Maybe you're an archer, Miss Elisabeth D. Canton, and not a future nurse! You've just never held a bow!

What I am thinking (in this incessant heat— however many days without rain, and three horses escaped!) is that I am destined for a destiny I haven't had the chance to meet. I am sure that if we had stayed longer in one of the many places where we lived, I would have met it. Perhaps I was meant to be a sheepherder, like those hardy men in England. I'm nothing if not patient. Or a pastry chef! No, not a pastry chef, I don't love sweets as you do, but surely you understand what I'm pointing to. How was it that you were able so early and so quickly to fall into what you love? I'm sure that I'd be a more "realized" person if I could have stayed in school!

For example, poetry. I quite liked studying that, you know. Maybe there is a poet inside of me who only needed a little bit more time before she understood the whole of everything, like when to move from one line to the next.

Or maybe I'm meant to be a mother, a better one than mine. Oh, I know you think she's dashing, but sometimes I want to <u>feel</u> her instead of see her moving in her silly hats. You know, to feel that she is listening, instead of shut up in her bedroom or collapsed hysterically with Antoine Legrand. I want to be bright and know things, I just want to know things! Instead I'm excelling at staying silent during conversation and sweating through my clothes. An instrument, at least, but we don't have our good

piano yet—it's somewhere in between the two of us
(if you're still in Hertfordshire!), floating on the
sea. Maybe there will be a tutor for me on the art
boat, smuggled after all. (You could hide there
also—wouldn't that be fun? Or wouldn't it be fun
once you arrived?) I'm eager also to learn Spanish,
but I'm embarrassed to ask the cook here, and in any
case, there are always things to cook.

So it's hopeless, you can see. Nothing for me to be
enterprising over, and of course everyone is old.
Sometimes I think that the best course of action
would be to walk out into the ocean and politely
drown. Not that being a great artist is so wonderful,
not like you would think it; you should see the faces
here! You'll remember Charlotte Hartsworth? The
one who rode without a saddle? She wrapped her
manuscript in palm leaves and asked the cook to
burn it, but Maria (she's the cook and she is lovely)
seems to know how feverishly minds change here,
so she didn't, and I was in the kitchen when C.
came back for it; she had tears when she saw that
she still could.

I will tell you one thing, though, that's different
than at home. I might have an *amigo*, as they say! Not
like <u>that</u>, of course, everyone is ancient, but what I
mean is there's finally an artist who's not fiddling

with my hair or looking at me like I'm a weeping
donkey of some kind. His name is Jack Klinger and
I don't have many details because I'm only just aware
of him and you don't go up haranguing people you've
just met. He used to be part of the "Dada" scene, I
gather, and lived with Mum in Vienna, by which I
mean "among" her crowd. I don't think they were
together, although as I'm writing this, I realize I
don't know for sure, but he strikes me as a little too
sensible for her, actually, so I probably can say that.
He lives out on a ranch here, and has little time or
interest in us although we can't say the same. (You
remember silly Hetty, don't you, Hetty of the rash-
ers? You should see her blush when Jack's around!)

Everything's been quite glum since he last visited
for dinner, and I'm thinking that I might go after
him to see what his own home is like, or perhaps
that I will paint it. He's a "Herr" by the way, older
even than Mum is, but it's hard to tell an age with
Germans, don't you think? Konrad's the same way,
really, he looks old and young at the same time.
Although he lost a lot of weight in the internment
camp, so even though the artists are in awe of him,
he isn't what he was.

Elisabeth, what else? If only we could lie out on
my balcony and look up at the sky. But we couldn't

do it as long as in England because the sun here is too hot. Speaking of great distances, I don't have to tell you that Mumma's in all states about her boat. She's put all her favorite art in it to get to Mexico, but it has to cross the Atlantic and get to Florida first. You do realize what could become of us should the collection actually sink? I could come to live with you, perhaps, wherever it is you are, and we would be like sisters, like we always said. With the way Mumma would feel about the collection gone, I'd be an orphan, more or less.

(On the subject of her Great Collection: you wouldn't believe how we were running about for it when we were back in France. Mumma had us hiding the important ones in the most rickety of barns, and then she gathered them all back up again because of rot and rain, but what with the waves and the salt, too, in the ocean, I'm not sure it wasn't wiser to keep them in those barns!)

It's true that it's exciting, and I know of all you think, but if your own mother were running around talking about putting a museum in a jungle where it's too hot to even think, I think you'd appreciate what your own is like, regardless of her shawls!

Well, I'd like to sign off by saying that I have something terrifically interesting to do, a Spanish lesson, for example, but I have nothing like that, and I lack, apparently, even the imagination to tell a pleasant lie, so I am going to go now and think about how to get this letter to you before the war arrives!

Your loving *amiga*,
Lara Calaway

Martes

Well you have to take things into your own hands, I guess, when it comes to diversions! I've started to wait for C. at the bottom of her hill. Her writing must be going terribly, for there are her footprints in the dirt: back and forth, up and down, up and down to the huge house.

The first time wasn't on purpose, really. I'd taken Hetty's garden book down to the bottom of the house entrance near the beginning of the jungle. Set a task for myself, actually: describe the things I saw. I wanted to use poetic language, to try and paint it on the page. I got:

A tiger behind the leaf stars (maybe! in the black)
Vines crisscrossing like fallen wires, green, deranged, engorged

That's all I got, and I was quite taken with it, when C. came down the path. Would you know, she actually seemed relieved to have me with her. Father, too, got lonely with the writing. That's why we had the dogs.

"Shall we walk?" she asked. We agreed to walk toward the stables, and picked up, for the both of us, great sticks, in case a crocodile should slide onto the path. (This has not happened to me, but it did on one of C.'s rides when Konrad wasn't with her. Her horse reared, of course, but she kept control of him. I trust that this is true because C. never talks about her experiences in a boastful way; she can be rather matter-of-fact about things, really.)

I am going to try to make an effort here to write down what we walked through, using Hetty's plant book. Prickled cherimoya fruit thudding to the ground and the pinkest Mexican crow flowers arrowing between trees, the same flowers, I have learned, that Ophelia either pretended to distribute in "Hamlet" or actually, truly did. Things can feel like that in Costalegre, real and invented at the same time. As in: What are flowers doing opened up like that in the winter, anyway?

An iron ring here, one there, to tether up the horses, but just this narrow path otherwise with its canopy of cypress and its too-dry dirt. All manner of insects working back and forth across it, the names for which even Cecile Matschat, in all her horticultural wisdom, does not have the words.

"You must be terribly bored here," C. said, as we walked. It's so exciting, really, not knowing what someone will say to you, and then it's said. "Or do you like the nature?"

"I do," I said. "I'm trying to learn." I held up the book that I was carrying, about the Mexican gardens. "It's Hetty's," I said to her raised eyebrows. "Research."

"I see." C. smiled. "And she isn't researching today?"

I felt the need to be protective of her, even if she is silly. Hetty had lent me the garden book, and the Spanish phrase one, after all.

"I think she's past the research bit."

"Of course."

We walked on.

As I'm back at Occidente now, I can just list out the things, without trying to describe them:

Daturas

Jacaranda

Stands of chestnuts

The pinkest pepper trees

Don't they sound more beautiful without me trying to place them in the place that I just saw? Because what do I know of them except that the jacaranda will turn purple when it blooms, and that we could probably eat the

chestnuts if we had carried them back with us. But it's
hard to know what is too intimate a gesture when you're
walking through the jungle with the woman your new
father prefers. Stooping to gather chestnuts is probably
such a one.

"So do you think that Jack will come around again?" I
tried to sound as if I was making conversation, but C. was
ever sly.

She smiled at me, visibly. "Not you too," she smirked.
Gallantly, she didn't make me answer. "He always was a
cat."

I didn't know what she meant by this, and I didn't want
her to catch me in my ignorance, so I didn't ask.

"Have you known him a long time?" I asked, which
seemed a perfectly reasonable question, but she was still
staring at me. Like that.

"On and off," she said. "As one does, with all the
moving. He was sent away, you know, banned, earlier than
the rest of us. Konrad and Jack both went to school with
Schlechty." She coughed, but held her hand up. "With the
Führer. But Jack's not interested in tact. Afraid he went
out of his way to point out how hopeless the Great Führer
was as an artist, how . . . tedious, you know? But some
people can't be teased. But then, I suppose it wasn't really
teasing. Jack probably smelled it, even then. How vengeful
he could be. How . . . mad. I think it was infuriating for

Schlechty to be around people who were gifted. And"—
she held her finger up, as if conducting her own thoughts—
"impertinent. Because Jack does it all, you know, collages,
drawings, painting . . . he even writes sometimes. But he
doesn't care. He used to. Painted for the war, I don't suppose you knew that?"

I let my throat make a muffled sound; I didn't want her
to stop talking.

"Official war artist. Can you imagine? Don't suppose
they'll have those this time round. Sent to the front lines
to paint."

C. stopped in her path and bent down to inspect a stick
insect that was either eating, or a part of, a green and spiny
leaf.

"That's how he got into Dadaism," C. said. "Nothing
meaning anything, all that. This was after the war. They
tried to show the world the senselessness . . ." She stroked
the insect's back. "He believed it for a while, Jack. He
really did. Back in Vienna, you should have seen what they
got up to." C. smiled, and stood up. Seemed determined
to continue, and oh, I had a thrill!

"They really believed. Fire, fire, fire. Got people
worked up about it, too. But then you had the clashes,
and the ludicrous inflation. Really, it turns out that
people just want to buy things, they don't want to change
their minds."

I watched as the stick insect reached the place where the dirt road turned to jungle to join the other leaf things in the woods.

"Anyway, everyone says he's done with making art. Which probably isn't true. If it were true, he'd be dead. Some people need to create in order to be whole. I hope . . ." Her face was troubled. "I hope he gets that back."

I could tell from the place her eyes were looking that she wasn't talking about Jack anymore. I wasn't immune to the talk; I'd lived in the houses, too. How something had broken inside Konrad at Les Milles, permanently taken. How it wasn't as liberating as the artists had thought it would be, to experience real fear.

"Well," I said, not wanting to venture into talk of Konrad, which would, in its own way, be talk about my mother, whom C. had once called "inconsequential" in front of me and Mum. "So you don't think he'll come around again?"

"Oh, sure," she said. "When he finds time. You know, Jack's not like the rest of us, sitting around banging our heads against the wall day after day for the right words. From what I gather, he lives like a real Mexican. Selling cattle, killing cattle, I don't know." She seemed rattled all of the sudden, and I feared it was my fault.

"But yes," C. said, as if she'd decided to be kinder. "It would be nice to do something. Really do something.

Something that's not this." Her gesture encompassed the walking, and also the waiting: the waiting for the boat to come, the waiting for the rain, the waiting for the time when she would be back to working proudly, without so many breaks.

"He's a special man, you know," C. said, her shoulders a bit higher. "He's never belonged to anyone. Never could be bought."

My cheeks burned. Who else could she be speaking of but Mum? And why would she, when we were having a nice talk? I had thought it obvious, almost like a rule even, that we wouldn't talk of Mum.

It is hardly worth noting that we didn't make it to the stables. Or that I didn't dare say anything further to the woman after that. How terrible! The closer my life gets to something consequential, there's always a reason, decorum, history, a suggestion to turn back.

I will have to learn to be bolder and stop swallowing my concerns! For example, I could have said: That is out of place! I realize about my mother and the things that people say, but Konrad would have starved to death if she hadn't married him, and now here he is. Worse for wear, and surely, but C. is here too, and it certainly isn't right to speak of a person's mother in a manner where things are said that aren't.

I find Charlotte appealing but she is also RUDE!

Lunes

Real news! Real news, at last. The National Socialists have taken Austria, so all is talk of Anschluss. A newspaper has been brought in from Vallarta: the Führer drove into his hometown in an automobile with over four thousand marching guards!

So now Austria and Germany are one again, and Baldomero is delighted. Not because of the Anschluss but because Mexico's at arms! Apparently Mexico is the only country that thinks the Anschluss isn't right, and Baldomero and Legrand couldn't be prouder to be here. Even Caspar has been caught smiling.

Baldomero says how thrilling it is to see a place with bite, and Legrand was moved nearly to tears while cheering this impossible country's fight against what he calls a "laziness of soul."

Struggle, struggle they say, is at the heart of it—you maintain your essentialism if you've never had a silver spoon, so of course now there is talk of letting go of the servants once again.

Mother is amused by the pride and fury: it's got the artists working. C.'s been writing feverishly, and Hetty's been up in her room with the door thrown open, weeping about the boat. She's sure that there will be war now and that a submarine will steal the paintings. She has no place to be worried but she's always been like that. Konrad hasn't been coming out of his room but Mum thinks it's a phase. Walter is sick with something, green-skinned, in bed most of the time. News paralyzes or catalyzes: I am learning more than the names of all the weeds.

Maria has been making stews and making them quite hot: she puts a separate bowl out for me, but the main stew's near inedible. I think she's trying to remind the artists what is really Mexican, but no one dares complain because they're so taken with the culture and the pride of it, right now. Mum's talking about organizing a mission to Puerto Vallarta for news about her boat, and also she has planned another dinner party; she wants it to be Mexican. She wants to celebrate the fact that we have come to the right place. She has sent Jose Luis out with a note to invite Jack over, so! I'm not sure which night it will be but won't that be quite grand.

Speaking of expeditions, Baldomero says there is no better time than now to find his little monkey. He says what with the large-scale work he is creating here, and the kinkajou he'll rescue, the Mexicans will probably hang his portrait above their beds and in their little shops, and that is why it is essential that he find his creature while the air is filled with pride.

Mother has pointed out to him that he's no more Mexican than she is; in fact, she is more Mexican, because she is a landowner, and Baldomero said his blood is filled with moons of Spanish rage.

Hura crepitans
The Early Gardeners

A most curious development, *Hura crepitans*, the sandbox tree (equally referred to in these parts as the possumwood, the jabillo, and the monkey-no-climb), is an evergreen of the spurge family that prefers partial shade and is often cultivated for this same want of shade.

Soaring to heights of up to sixty meters, the sandbox is covered in pointed spines and smooth bark (very prized for furniture-making if one can rid the wood of spikes). The red flowers never petal, though a peculiar fruit is all the same produced, a volatile fruit known to spontaneously erupt when ripe, throwing its seeds as far as 100 meters at speeds of 250 kilometers per second. The sound produced at these explosions is very well near dynamite, and one would be advised to stay on the side of this curmudgeonly creation where the seeds aren't being thrown.

I have been told that the sap from the sandbox is both milky and poisonous, and that indigenous fisherman coat their fishhooks with this poison. Arrow tips can also be dipped into this substance, so one is struck, as one is learning of the sandbox, that it is an ultimate foolishness to brave the jungle alone.

Jueves

New father is working on a painting. Mother woke me with the news. I don't go into his studio, not the one in Mexico. The ones in the other houses have been harder to avoid.

Mother is flattered, delighted, thrilled. She pulled me up in my nightdress, said Konrad had gone out horseback riding, celebrating, no doubt, and that we should celebrate too. That the darkness might be leaving him. That it was quite a piece.

I've never liked going into the artist's studio without the artist present. It feels for all the world like you are looking at the absent person's entrails. Or sitting in their mind. It's far more polite and comfortable when the maker is there with you, staring at something huge and frightening that even he doesn't understand. The artist will always laugh or spill what they are drinking and say this or that thing about what it is they've done this time to keep the work from being right.

Konrad's studio is in a vacant room that is circular, like mine, but on the second floor. The walls are white and the wooden shutters were closed, which made the light seem mauve. From the orientation of the house, I knew that there was a view of the ocean, and that if I moved to the window (and pulled open the shutters), I just might see C. and Konrad riding on the beach, which is when it also occurred to me that perhaps it was mother who had pulled those shutters closed.

There were canvases of all sizes leaning against the walls, some not even stretched yet, some sloped to the ground. Because of the circular shape of the room, the canvases seemed to crowd you even though they were turned the other way. It was strange to see so many empty paintings in a room already white. At home, at whatever home, there were always paintings: paint drying, paint dripping, attempts in all directions, wooden furniture painted when Konrad had painted everything else.

But here. Only a few things. A yellow shape doing a somersault, a woman like a fruit peel. A forest of calf spines. Brushstrokes that didn't lead to anything at all.

In the center of the room, though, pinched upon an easel: the thing Mum had brought me in there for. "A bridal robing," Mum said, barefoot of feet and smile. "Incredible," she continued, with her small hand on her heart. "One of his very best."

My feet were also bare and the tile floor was cold. It was early. There were no other footfalls, no voices calling out. Just mother and the cold floor and the terrifying thing.

Four figures. Four figures leaving the chasm of some room. A mirror behind them, the floor black and white checkers, a serpentine column to the right. On the left, a bird guard: a swan the color of gangrene with human hands holding a rusted arrow across the bridegroom's groin, and this figure, the bride, a pale and lengthy human, legs endless, breasts pulsing, her face and shoulders covered in a red veil made of feathers and the widest-open eyes. Bird eyes, and a bird beak tangled up inside: the cloak fell to the floor around her, the effect of it like something ruined that has been left to decompose, and her nudity inside it. To the bride's right, a lady-in-waiting, also naked, belly swelling, breasts swelling, her hair half made of eyeballs, facing the opposite direction from the guard. The bride as if blinded, a palm out to find purchase, but there is only the protruding breast of her companion, absconded in some task. But near her feet, nearly <u>at</u> her feet if the guard chooses not to steer her, a gruesome girl gnome, pregnant and distended, rubbing a green fist into her tears.

Mother clapped. "Isn't it fantastical?" she swooned. "Look how well he's painted me! The legs, just as slim as mine are, and the stomach, exceptionally flat. Especially compared to this figure here." She pointed to the lady-in-waiting, whom I suspected to be C. "How embarrassing. I'm so pleased!"

Mother never expects me to comment on the paintings, to say they're good or bad. She needs a witness to hear her call them something that they aren't. And then that's what's said in public. That will be the impression that is decided on.

I've been in Konrad's paintings before, the one where Mum had a horse head and a robe of organs. I know which figure I was because the hair was my hair. I was facing out to sea. I had on a nightshirt that stopped above my buttocks, and then nothing, not until the robin-blue slippers that used to be my favorites, the ones with the gold bows.

Of that piece, Mum told everyone that her likeness took up most of the space in the painting, that it was the largest one with the most elaborate brushstrokes, the robe of organs she was wearing, very complicated to paint. She said it showed Konrad's loyalty, to include us as a family in such a large-scale work.

You are supposed to forget these things. You are not supposed to think into them. But they do come for you, the pink cleft, the blue shoes.

Lunes

Nothing good can come from lunch. This is one of mother's sayings, but Jack could only come for lunch, and men can't fish at night. So everyone assembled at two thirty, pulled from work, or hate.

We were back to stagnancy. The heat, as yet unbroken; the news, no news; the rain that teased to fall at any time, and then (truly teasing) didn't.

Over the weekend, another horse gone from the stables. At night there are dark sounds, like a kind of heaving. Not neighs or whimpers, these are the cries of animals who are going to escape.

When Jack arrived for luncheon, even his own horse was like something tracked. Ears pinned, his bead eyes wide. Nostrils huge and desperate. No good can come at day.

Konrad found out that mother saw the painting and had been complimenting him to everyone. Boasting that he'd "returned." As a punishment, he has stopped working, or he has been unable to. He said he took a knife to the canvas, but I don't think he did. A knife to mother is more likely, now that we're all here to watch.

I helped Maria make another flan but it wasn't gay this time. Monday is usually a rest day, so none of the staff are happy. I don't know why it had to be Monday, or fish, but it did, and so it was. Maria wasn't humming as she normally does, a sung word from time to time, she just clucked at me, and then the head shaking, and I want to say, I'm fine! I'm here after all, I'm cooking with you, I am not my father's darkness, I didn't do those things. Sometimes, this day, I just want to be a child in a pink house on the beach, with English books to get through, my own friends to play with, sand and yellow cornmeal underneath our fingernails.

I changed for lunch. Who cares. Sometimes it feels as if my beauty is this expected thing I must show up with, so I try not to, but I guess I'm vain, as well. I didn't want my mother to whine about how she would have preferred the white dress to the pink one, how my hair shouldn't be bunned. Even Baldomero puts his word in: says when my hair's down, that it's striking. Legrand reaches for it, runs it through his stubby fingers. A treasure, he says. An international one.

Jack was late, and so the loons started one of their old games down by the pool. Hetty in a swimsuit, her shapely calves stretched out, and Legrand kneeled down before her, painting lines around her toes.

"I'm a zebra!" Hetty yelped. She'd had wine; the others also. Pitchers kept on coming out; Maria's mouth was pinched.

I was sitting underneath the palapa, reading my big book about the native scenery, which is tiring me some. The author is so taken by her world of plants, completely absorbed by it, always eating fruit. Always in some nice locale eating lovely fruit. Her life dedicated to the task of writing these plants down. How terribly wicked to be so single-minded. And fortunate for her.

Baldomero came and sat by Hetty, brought a brush up to her thigh. My mother said something that made everybody laugh, but I didn't hear what.

Hetty had a big hat on; she was pleased with her appearance. C. was already half naked in the pool. Mum once said the first time she encountered C., she'd come to a drinks party completely naked with the soles of her feet painted in yellow mustard, left tracks all through the house. I both believe this and don't believe it. But I suppose it's true.

When Jack arrived, Baldomero was wielding his brush around Hetty's groin, and I was pretending to be absorbed by my big book. Maria slouching when she was rung for more red wine.

The property was in a state again. Perhaps because it wasn't nighttime, mother hadn't gone to a great effort, and the litter from their other games was in the pool. A wilted paper lantern. A small table on which me and Walter had played cards. C. floating belly up with her breasts out, nipples to the sun like cherries on an *île flottante*, which is something I thought before Legrand actually said it, calling, "Maria, Maria, can we whip some cream! Our île flottante is floating!!" And everybody laughed. It would take a very clever person to diagram what the loonies think is fun.

Jack stood there with his bird face. Not everyone was there. Walter had long since stopped coming to meals with us, instead Mum had them trayed out to him, and I had only the sight of dirtied dishes to prove he wasn't dead. Caspar was in the bushes, trying to catch a certain insect whose name I have forgotten, but it has a bright blue back and teethed antennae, and he has been making photographs of these insects using only water, shade, and sun. Ferdinand had been there earlier, but he wasn't at that moment. He had taken to going on long walks across Teopa, gathering more rocks.

The group saw Jack. My mother threw her hand up in a wave, and Jack's body stayed uneasy, which made my mother laugh.

Konrad was there also, in a palm chair near the pool. White trousers, white shirt opened all the way to his

navel, too thin, but not ashamed about it like he'd been
before, his skin the kind of tan that no one else's turned.
And hairless, like a boy.

"I'm not eating an orgy," Jack said. "You invited me to
lunch."

"Oh, talk, talk, talk, talk, talk," said mother, rolling to
her back. "You're tremendously late, you know."

"Three of my cows got out. This weather." I watched
him take his hat off. "If only it would rain."

"More scorpions for us!" said Baldomero, peeling himself off Hetty. "I've quite a collection. You should see the
guts. Have you seen their guts?" He made a sound as if he
were choking. And then he produced a feather from the
clutches of his cape and started tickling Hetty's toes.

"I'm not in the mood for this," said Jack. "Are we having
lunch?"

His head turned in the direction of the galley kitchen
behind the palapa, where the food came out. His face
didn't change when he saw me, which made me feel foolish. Maria was probably not going to come out again, not
till they rang the bell for lunch.

So I rose, even though I felt unwanted, and asked if I
should fetch her. I wanted to say something, after all.

"Ha! She gets up for him! What about the rest of us? It's
mutiny in the kitchen!" This was Baldomero, whose face
was sweating now.

"Hallo, Heinrich," C. singsonged from the pool, where she was swimming slow laps backward, never hitting the side once.

I watched her arms cut through the water. I could see her armpits. I dared a look at Jack because she'd called him Heinrich.

"You truly are degenerates," is what Jack said.

"Oh please," said mother, pulling her skirt up to twirl her toes at him. "You used to be one too."

I want to tell the stories. The ones that can't be real. Here is a story that Magda used to tell me. Magda, she of the "Go to sleep, *cariños*" and the warm pieces of bread.

In the mountains there are women called the *Ciguapa*, naked except for their own manes. Their feet face backward, and the people who try to trap them lose their sanity sorting out which way their tracks travel. If you look a *Ciguapa* in the eye, you are eternally transfixed. Many travelers are transfixed on the mountains. They die of fear, and cold.

What if I held everything inside of me? What if you couldn't tell which way my tracks went?

Lunes?

Here is another story. My brother was in Mexico with us, those years ago, last time. Mother was married to our father: the first, the writing one. We stayed in the pink house on the water on top of a pink beach. There was a restaurant on the beach called the Playa Rosa. We lunched there every day. The restaurant was filled with people, including the famous moviemaker who started up this place. It was loud and they were happy, people rubbing our heads telling us, "Adorable, so sweet."

We would go out with the American to watch his men catch fish. He would let us take the mildewed life vests off once we were out of mother's sight. Here is the story. One day, my brother begged, could he go swimming. The American just laughed. I watched my brother hesitate on the side of the small boat. We knew what kinds of things were swimming underneath us because we had seen them pulled out of the water, fighting, always fighting, to stay inside the sea.

My brother jumped that day. And almost drowned. Of course he did—he'd never swum before. But what I remember most isn't the American jumping in for him, his man cutting the motor; it's my brother smiling as he jumped into the ocean. The beauty of that first time that was only his.

He wasn't scared, you know. We told the American never to tell our mother and I don't think that he did. But that night, and all of the other nights in the casita, Stephan would clasp his hands to my shoulders and whisper to me desperately, "Did you see what I did?"

Martes

The argument started about the Anschluss. Walter had actually joined us by then, looking more tired than sick. He said his family would be jailed. Surely—the Führer had so many in his army—they'd know about the papers he had forged by now, that there had been too many, that he'd been a fool to come.

"Can't we start off with something more lighthearted?" Mother asked. "You're here. We're all out. As soon as that fellow's back from Puerto Vallarta, he'll fix his telegram. Or I'll send Eduardito to Puerto Vallarta. We'll all go on a trip."

"I have no way of knowing," Walter protested. "We have no way of knowing. I don't know if they're all right."

"And I have no way of knowing whether my boat has sunk," said mother. "We can only know what's before us. And, well." She snorted. "Even then."

"We shouldn't be here," said Caspar, who hadn't found his bug.

"And where would you have us be?" Mum asked. "What a dreadful lot you are! Rosa, shan't we have some margaritas? Isn't that more gay?"

"Her name is Maria," said Jack, who wasn't drinking wine. I flushed because I knew this, and had said it, but hadn't insisted publicly, which was the same as never saying anything at all.

"We must start over, really. No talk of anything that we can't be happy of," insisted Mum. "Have you heard that Konrad's made a masterpiece? Jack, you have to see it. Surely, it's his best."

"It isn't finished," said fake father. "And it wasn't ready to be seen."

"And yet we saw it, and we were absolutely charmed by it. Weren't we, Lara?"

Everyone turned to watch what I would do with my face and with my words. Even, I'll note, Konrad.

"I don't know," I answered, feebly. "If it wasn't ready . . . "

"But that's the entire point! They paint it, and we see it," mother said. "Art is to be seen. Otherwise we'd have the stuff in coffins instead of in museums. I'm sure it's his best, and I'm sure it will fetch a happy price."

"From you?" Legrand laughed. "Or me?"

"*Genug*!" shouted Konrad, banging down a fork. "Must you always, always, <u>always</u> talk of price? Do you know how tiresome you are? Do you know how little anyone here enjoys you? Just this morning, at the stable, I saw those shining bits and I thought, God above, wouldn't it be glorious if—"

"So you believe in God now?" asked mother, cutting fish. "Came close enough to death for that?"

"Oh!" cried Hetty, clutching her napkin. "I thought we would be light!"

"Why don't we just eat," said C., "while we still have food."

"Don't be morose, darling," crooned mother. "The war's not coming here."

"We are the war, you imbecile," spat Konrad. "No amount of fucking flounder will change the fact that you're a Jew."

Jack pushed his chair from the table. "Enough. I know that decency is beyond you, but to speak like this in front of a child—"

"Oh, Lara's not a child," went Konrad. "Look at her." He threw his hand out. "Look."

"She is a child," said Jack, not looking. "And she shouldn't be exposed to your disgusting games. Where is her brother? Where is her father? What is wrong with you?"

Jack was staring at my mother now, whose hands were folded over her plate.

"Oh, please!" cried Hetty. "I beg you! It's such a lovely lunch!"

"It was," said mother, wiping at her lip line with an ironed napkin. "I find your interest in child-rearing positively fascinating. For a runaway married to cows."

"Well, you ran right after me, didn't you?" asked Jack. "We're all a bunch of cowards."

"I, for one, find it much more gay to be alive," said mother, reaching for the bell as she was out of wine. "And if I'm alone in this, we can arrange for passage back for those of you who find peacetime insulting. Although I daresay that the food and drink will be more . . . sparse."

"You are a disgusting woman," said Konrad, standing. "And I ruined my life by joining it with yours."

At the top of the driveway, we all heard it. The boom of it, then shrill. Jack's horse had gotten out.

Wildflowers of Mexico

Tropical succulents will bloom readily in our temperate climate, but many of them are frost-haters and must be taken indoors at the first suspicion of cold weather. But they do furnish a wealth of glorious material.

A rock garden is supposed to resemble a bit of a mountainside.

Probably hardy even in our cold, wet winters, *Draba mexicana* should be placed in well-drained soil in full sun and must be well matured by the autumn. Propagation is by division or seed, sown in either spring or fall.

Colonial Gardens

In every lonely solitude there stands a church, whose tiled domes gleam against the towering volcanoes.

The gardens of Mexico are different from all others in the world!

Miércoles

Lunch ended at that, of course. Konrad poured his wine out and I sat there blankly as it pooled onto the wooden floor. Mother didn't say anything, even though our feet got splashed.

Then Konrad left us, I guess for Teopa. C. followed, refusing any discretion. Mum sat and ate her fish while Jack edged onto one of the deserted chairs and spoke to her, too quietly for the rest of us to hear. I had hopes for their conversation. All the things he wanted! Perhaps the best artist is an old artist; he can finally wish for something pleasant to occur for someone else. He would convince Mum to send Papa and Stephan over. He would convince her: school. I'd have books and I could name things, paint all the pictures in the world.

But mother slid her silverware back and forth into her fish. Jack pulled away from the table. And I knew he'd given up. There was no other way for it to end, really. She only listens to Konrad. But still. She had shared some youthfulness with Jack.

Hetty sobbed into her meal and Baldomero asked Caspar to have the rest of his meal sent to his room, as exposure to stupidity gave him indigestion.

Walter and Jack looked at one another. Walter, who used to have such friendly, teasing eyes.

"She shouldn't be here," Jack said. But he said this to Walter.

Walter closed his lips together. His yellowing eyes said, "No."

Well I could barely breathe for all of this, and my mother chewing the whole time. Her wine was not the one tipped over, so she sipped and sipped. Chewing each bite repeatedly. I wanted to cry for it. And plus I was hungry. My mind was like a balloon sent up into the sky.

Jack tried once more before leaving. "Leonora," (this was softly) "you can't continue this."

And my mother: "I think it's you who can't."

Jack stood and put his hat on. My heart wanted to shout. Was there really nothing you could say to change someone? Could words never hurt enough? But she'd been hurt. We'd seen it. Father stepping on her stomach, howling that she was empty-headed, borrowed other people's tastes.

I hoped for something miraculous, and of course it didn't come. Jack had on his hat by then. He didn't look at me. But it maybe stayed with me longer, the not looking, than it might have if he had.

Hetty started sobbing louder and Mum complained that it was impossible to enjoy one's meal in these conditions and hauled Hetty toward her room.

It was me and Walter then. I don't feel like I should write this, because he's always been so nice to me, but Walter was crying too.

Ferdinand arrived. I don't know where he'd been or what he had seen of all of this. He sat down between Walter and me. He looked back and forth between the both of us. And then, in front of my left hand, which was curled into a fist, he placed one gray, one pink, and one shining silver rock.

Viernes

To give order to our days, Legrand has set up dream briefs and automatic drawings. I know, because he boasts about it, that Legrand was once a medical student, and that he worked in the neurological ward during the Great War. So he thinks he has a way with soldiers, or people with dark times.

Legrand says that society has reduced our dream life to "parentheses," and that to be fully liberated (creatively and artistically) we must put more of the unconscious into conscious life.

The dream briefs take place under the palapa, in slots during the morning. Baldomero doesn't participate because his whole life is a dream brief, but for everyone else it's an hour of telling Legrand what you dreamt about, and then drawing the associations from the dreams you saw.

Legrand hangs up the automatic drawings on a clothesline around the palapa so that everyone can see whose dreams are worse. It was C. who went this morning. A headless woman with her arm cast through a sea urchin, her fist with a grenade. There was a red object in the right-hand corner of her drawing, but I couldn't tell what it was supposed to be because it finally rained today, and all the colors bled.

Dear Stephan,

Do you remember when we went to see the cliff divers last time we were here? Do you think you could ever take a dive as long as that?

Day?

Mother went today. For the dream brief. Her drawing was a sailboat. There was an earring too. Legrand told her she wasn't exploring her subconscious. What does he know? Mother's always dreaming, anyway.

Dwellers in the Sun

One of the most gorgeous of all the lovely *Cerei* tribe is a half-wild species known as *Junco espinoso* or the snake cactus, *Nyctocereus serpentinus.* The long, clinging tentacles, growing in dense twisted and twining clusters, remind one of long, slender tropical snakes waiting patiently beside the jungle trail for their prey. Supposedly a native of Mexico's eastern coastal section, it clambers over hedges, walls, and cliffs, perfuming the night with its spicy fragrance. The stems, about an inch in diameter, grow erect for a few feet, then bend over in a prostrate fashion and run along any support upon which they can get a foothold. The spines are weak and flexible, a creamy white and brown, with darker tips.

Gardens of the Ancients

Previous to this ceremony, no smelling of the flowers was allowed.

Martes

I am in trouble for my dream brief. Legrand says I'm not going deep enough. What was drying on the clothesline: three riderless horses, running on the beach toward the massive *copa* that the American installed, a structure of cement that looks like a huge mooncup, an offering for rain.

"This isn't how you would have dreamt it," Legrand said of my wet papers. "All of this exists. Try again," he said, handing me more paper, the charcoal dusted on his skin and mine.

"But that's what I dreamt."

"I know what's happening with you," he said, bending lower, "and this isn't what you dreamt."

I bit my bottom lip hard between my teeth to keep my stupid chin from trembling. What is the worst about Legrand is that he's been there all along. He knows whether I was wanted. He knows whether I am now. He knows everything, sees everything, ruins everything, he is the reason she is restless, her restlessness is the reason we can't stay in any house, and why father couldn't stay with us, he who just wanted to write in his study, and all the drinks at night.

I dreamt of a carafe filled with feces and red wine.

I dreamt of Maria with her face on backward. Her hair down to her waist.

I dreamt of the larders emptied except for her black hair.

I dreamt of a figure marching on a bloated stomach. Red cloak on the ground.

"I only dreamt the horses," is what I said to Antoine Legrand.

Viernes

The door to my room is still only made of fabric. Things fly in through the round window that I cannot name. In the morning, if I walk out on the terrace, the white whales crest and spout. I am painting. I am painting quite a lot. I am painting the true things that I dream about.

Lunes

More papers, and by that I mean real news. All of the German people are united into one country. The top jobs have been given to the *Nationalsozialismus*, and a man named Seyss-Inquart is now the Minister of the Interior. Mother paid heaps to have the news brought from Vallarta, and I drew the name into the things I'm painting, like one of Konrad's old collages where paint was mixed with fact.

Seyss-Inquart. Too many *s*'s and strange letters, *y*, *i*, *q*. At the table, when the newspaper was shown to us, Walter said the name in German and my skin bumped into goose freckles. Even in this heat.

Jewish Austrians are washing the streets with handfuls of torn clothing; there was a photo of this too. Men, women, and even children, on their knees, and it is winter. The streets would be wet, you know, so it's even colder for their knees.

"You'll all thank me later," is what my mother said.

Tardes—más? (is later?)

Mother went to Puerto Vallarta as she'd half-promised, with Legrand and Baldomero and Caspar, for a few days. She received word that her boat left France, but had no confirmation of where the boat was now, nor whether her paintings and her people had made it—would make it—to Saint Augustine. And of course, all the things that could go terribly between Florida and us.

And we have a telegram from father: "Switzerland's unmovable. Skiing's fine. All my love to Flossy—H."

Flossy is what he calls me, because of my dumb hair. Not a word about my brother. For a man who builds his life on letters, he never did know what to write. My seasons are filled with such gray missives from my father:

"Water bluer than ever at the Cap. Tremendous fish!"

"Writing well. Stephan playing rugby. All my love to F!"

"Considering an animal. Berner Sennenhund? (Too Swiss?)"

In mother's absence, Hetty gossips. "Did you know that Charlotte was saved from the Great War by submarine?" she asks. "They sent a nanny in a submarine. She's very, very rich."

When she tells me this, I imagine a uniformed woman standing at a boat's prow, even though I know that in real life she would be underwater, that a submarine doesn't have a prow. I try to imagine C. as a child, but I only see myself.

Miércoles

People are missing their appointments for their dream briefs, so Legrand is revising his Surrealist Manifesto, again.

"You try to pause creation, but every night we dream!" he exclaimed one night at dinner. (Fish.) "And so it is that we must work our bones to access dreams during the day! Discipline is the complement of a wild mind! The seeing mind is fire and the sleeping mind is hay!"

My father used to tell me that Antoine Legrand was an intolerable person and a gifted poet, as most poets are. "A pen in hand temps misery from its shadows," was something Legrand wrote once. My father kept it on his desk. My father writes and writes but he hasn't published yet.

The last time Legrand revised this document he called for the excommunication of all surrealists who didn't believe in Collective Action. "Surrealism at the Service of the Revolution!" it was called. He wrote it in our home in

Paris, mother even let him write key phrases on the wall, where they'd later hang the phrase about the "thrash" from the director of the Louvre. When he'd finished his revision, a great party was held and a list was made of the unfaithful. The faithful are all here.

"At heart, he's just a child who has to buy his playmates," I once heard father say.

. . .

Mother is back and has a headache, so Hetty plays Legrand's secretary down at the pool.

"We no longer live under the reign of logic!" Legrand shouts.

"There is a hatred of the marvelous!"

"SURREALITY is the absolute reality, the only place to live!"

When I came down for breakfast, Maria was rolling dough underneath a banner. "ALL HAIL THE OMNIPOTENCE OF THE AWFUL DREAM!"

Sábado

Konrad did a dream brief that turned into a painting. I watched my mother and Legrand pluck it from the clothesline. And mother chirping her head about it. Look how fine a thing.

Blue sky. The wall of a house, Mexican pink, and two squares cut like windows without glass. A white hand stretching through one of the cut out windows, knuckle-less, long fingers crossed round a red ball. From the ball, a string that winds up and down the wall of the bright house. A stick insect is climbing. Two palm trees that look like asparagus growing beyond the wall. The hand's fingers, more like legs.

Underneath this, lines:

The road is not impassable
When you say to,
it begins.

The grass is full of sparrows
the first youth is closed.

Legrand said that this one should not stay up on the clothesline. I watched them from the stairs, mother standing in front of the picture as if protecting a small child.

"He's humiliating you," said Legrand.

"He's making beauty because of me. His world is filled with beauty."

"I'm afraid you underestimate him."

"And he's underestimated me."

And in my stomach, sickness. To understand not everything, but to understand enough. Mother is never going to turn my door into a door.

And so I took the smallest horse. "The first youth is closed." How ridiculous to ask permission, even to escape. I could not saddle him myself. And the groom pointing to the sky, protesting, giving names to things. "*Tormenta. Tormenta!*" So much better than our "storm."

Well, I felt right, there in that saddle. The groom— against his wishes—drew directions in the sand. He talked of the *tormenta*, but I did not descend. My mother, after all, is known by everybody here. As are her caprices.

On the road, I cried for the heroic men. All the ones I've heard of. Grandpapa in his black tuxedo, in the rising seas. The Austrians pushing newspapers under-neath their children's knees while they scrub the frozen streets. But no heroes have ever come for me. My brother didn't yell when we were told that we'd live separately. Now father sends short letters and summers where there's shrimp. And I really am a stupid child to have hoped for stupid Jack.

The pony neighed and whimpered on the path out through the jungle. It was close to his evening meal and I was a fool to take him with the sky like that, but what of it? I've spent my whole life agreeing that I'm delicate, and what has come of that?

There really is a cement bowl here, built by the Americans as an offering for giants, rolled, I don't know how, onto a cliff above Teopa. I climbed it last time with Papa and with Stephan (mother's ankles too weak for the wooden stairs). There is an opening at the top of it to get into the bowl. Stephan squeezed through it and then Papa and I followed, and we were in the bowl then, and there wasn't any sound. I couldn't hear the ocean even though it was right there. It was like the bowl was holding me, like nothing bad could come. I remember Stephan ruining the quiet. Singing songs from boys' school, saying there wasn't any echo. Did we? Did we hear?

Well what girl doesn't dream of running free next to the ocean, but I didn't even have the courage to make the small horse gallop. The sand was harder than usual, and I thought if he started I might not be able to get the horse to stop, so we just plodded along on the beach toward the massive copa, the waves making my horse nervous, the wind making him nervous, and no birds in the sky.

If anyone was on the terraces of Occidente, they would have seen me on Teopa, right before a storm. Perhaps if the wind blew hard enough, the giant bowl would topple. Can you imagine the bowl floating across the ocean, passing all the people fleeing Europe, passing Mumma's boat?

I imagined it rolling over them, pressing all the artists down into the reefs, the paintings and our piano sinking past the eyeless fish. That is what I dream of. Eyeless things that drown.

> Dear Stephan, I thought, as the hooves sunk into sand, it's been too long since we've laughed.

At the first roll of thunder, the horse's ears pinned. Black clouds moving behind the ocean like enormous curtains. At the first slash of lightning, he reared, and I lost my stirrup. At the second one, he ran.

Sábado

I came to on one of the roadways, the strips of sand and dirt that look like all the other paths here, no difference between right or left or black. The stars were overhead and the air was filled with winged things on boughs. If I hadn't been so hurt I would have been more frightened. The long and clinging serpents. Insects hung on flesh.

I will admit something here that I'll never tell to anyone. I did see our house. How could I not, Occidente blazing at all hours, like something being filmed? I saw the blue house on the hilltop and I walked the other way. Even though it hurt most terribly to walk.

The pain was lessened by my imagining the groom's panic when the horse came back without a rider. He would call on my mother, try to get someone to understand that it hadn't been his fault. That I had insisted. My mother would finally cry for me, probably in public. Maria, maybe, too.

At the same time, I was embarrassed to imagine the horse running by himself. Charlotte would never let herself be thrown from a small horse! And in the jungle, of

all places! I listened to the screeching insects and waited
for the sound of the seeds that would explode. One of the
exploding fruits could come for me, could come right for
my head. The dark was even ghastlier when you weren't
on horseback. And of course, the silent snakes.

I'll admit another thing. Even for the scratches on my
back and knees, which at times throbbed or burned, I
wasn't actually frightened until the rain started. I figured
I could face anything if I wasn't cold—

> Dear Stephan,
>   How many letters have I tried here? And I still
> can't write my way to brave!

> Dear Elisabeth,
>   Did you want to be a daughter? Who gives you
> the choice?

> Dear Elisabeth,
>   What way is there, really, for you to stay my friend.

The truth is worse than what I've tried to make it: I was
thrown onto the beach. I was thrown and I hadn't even
been riding half the hour. As I lay on my back with the
pain thudding all through me, I remembered what an
instructor had said when I was small, that I had to hold

the mane if a horse reared. Of course this information came to me when it was too late to use it.

From the beach, though, I saw lanterns going at a hut, swinging from the wind, probably; I was too far away to see. It was the turtle man's. Mum let me and Stephan come out to see his hatchlings, the last time we were here. And even though no one is here who was here then, I guess the turtles are, and they need the man to watch them. We got to help them, the little turtles, scatter across the beach. It's very simple, horribly: they are born and they either make it or do not make it to the sea. The turtle man told us that the sea is not the predator, that we must watch the sky. That it's the birds who are most dangerous. We waved our arms and shouted so that they couldn't land.

So it was the turtle man who found me, with the English that he had. I had pain, but I insisted that I didn't because I felt so foolish. When he asked me what had happened, where I'd come from, I heard my voice say, "Señor Jack."

My horse hadn't run far, he said. There was grass behind his shack. The turtle man said he'd ride home with me. I said home was Señor Jack's.

Steph

Steph-Steph

The disappearing man

I could have asked whether he remembered the first jam.
Or that it had been from the tomatoes, the tomatoes we
had grown.

Do you remember how we helped Papa tie the tomato
branches back and the smell like basil and bright sun? We
used Mum's old stockings to do it and a stake. How Mum
said that nothing would grow in England, but those tomatoes did.

How the jam didn't turn out right. The smell wasn't
right either. That mother doesn't like waste so we had to
eat it with our breakfasts and our dinners for a while. The
color was a festive one but I didn't like the seeds. They
looked like small blond animals looking down their nose.

I don't know if it was the taste of it, or the fact that a lot
of the tomatoes did end up having blight, probably that
was it, probably it was because Mum had been right about

the growing, but real father rubbed jam into her hair that night and she thought it a joke. It became a test, later. She would sit for it, you know, just sit for it, even when other people told Papa to stop.

"L'nora!" he would shout, quoting from his favorite poet while he rubbed. "They catch the shrieks in cups of gold!"

Sábado

Everything was a little blurry with my head hurt and the storm, but I remember (I know that I remember this!) that Jack didn't startle when he found us at his gate. They spoke in Spanish, he and the turtle man. I like to imagine that Jack asked if I was hurt. They looked back and forth at me as if coming to a decision. They must have decided, not.

The thunder was still thundering and the heat lightning flashed. There was a fence running from the property: thick branches erected vertically and crossrails white as ghosts. The leaves tossing up and the branches also, ready for the quench.

I think Jack invited the turtle man to stay, but I don't think the turtle man had time to think about it. With Jack's help, which I needed, I had already dismounted, and the turtle man was working hard to keep his own frightened horse in place. Behind Jack's cabin, his own horses were stampeding, causing ours to rear. Things were getting out of hand for the poor man who had helped me; his horse was semicircling desperately, eyeing where to bolt. The turtle man gave in to him with a shout, galloping away from us so quickly, the horse's hooves barely touched the road.

"Let's get your horse settled, first off," Jack said, speaking to my mount, who he was holding, hard. Jack nodded behind him to the cabin. "You wait inside."

I looked guiltily toward the house.

"Just go inside," he said.

Jack's place isn't done in the Costalegre style. Most of the houses here are pastel-colored; Jack's is white with a tin roof. And small. But lots of land beyond it, mostly scrub, I think, or savannah's what it's called.

I could hear his cattle braying, the sound like something scraping back and forth across an empty floor. And the horses' hooves, an army. I'd heard that horses scream, but I'd never heard it happen. The sound was very female. I can't describe that sound. I could barely open the front door, my hands were shaking so.

Feeling the impostor, I stood for Jack's return. The door shut behind me because the wind had started up. As I hadn't been invited, it didn't feel right to notice how he had or hadn't fixed things, so I stared at the packed floor of the entrance and tried to think of nothing. But that didn't work because without something to fix my eyes on, I started feeling through the various humiliations that had brought me to Jack's house, so the only distraction from my loathing was to look at what he had.

There was a queer table against the wall in front of me, made out of what must have once been a log. It was a strange shape; maybe it was a sculpture, you certainly couldn't put anything on that table without it sliding off. Even the lanterns were placed next to it, unlit, on the floor. Jack held the only one with light.

From where I was standing, the cabin seemed one room, although I saw a curtain in a corner, blowing inward, an indication of something else behind. A window must be open, but I wasn't going to do anything about shutting it, wasn't going to do anything unless I was told to.

Because of the wall in the entranceway, I couldn't see around it to the rest of the small room, and I didn't dare to try. Alone and waiting in his house, with Jack having to settle a horse I'd nearly lost, I felt every inch of the burden I had caused. The shock of my fall, too, which had my body cold.

Jack came in and shook his coat off, water slicking from him. In his absence, the rain had shifted to something frightening, hard as apples, new ones, crashing to the roof. I couldn't hear the horses and I couldn't hear the cows. Behind me, I could feel the tilted table lilting to the side.

Jack hung his hat on a peg above me.

"Don't stand by the door," he said, picking up his lantern by the odd-shaped table. He walked into the main room and I heard him force the shutters closed. These sounds, at least, were things that I had lived with. Up at Occidente, I'd seen Mumma push against them with her shoulder to get her shutters closed.

"Care to help?" he called. I couldn't see him for the darkness. I followed him by sound, and then my eyes adjusted. A cookstove in the corner, wood piled to the right of it, a narrow bed against a wall. The sound, and then the smell, of Jack lighting another lantern.

"Just yank them closed, and bolt them. You've closed windows before?"

My cheeks burned as I tried to pull the pair closest to me shut with the little I could see. They were heavy and the wood was swollen, I couldn't get them sealed. Even with the bolt in place, the rain bounced and sputtered, puckling the sill with bulging drops. The rain was so noisy Jack had to yell his questions, and I didn't like his yells.

With the windows as closed up as they could be, the cabin was immersed in a new and stiller kind of darkness save for the yellow of the candles Jack had lit. There was an iron chandelier above a little table, and the table was positioned in the oddest manner. Or rather, the chandelier was. But once Jack had lit up all the candles sticking from the fixture, I understood the placement. All across the tables were scrapbooks, no, sketchbooks, with lovely leather covers. Huge ones, oversized, pages open, some hanging on top of other ones, like they were sleeping things. I tried not to look down, of course, but I could make out landscapes, modern landscapes, the way the artists do them, more feeling than the facts of what you see. Reds and whites and trees without any leaves left on their branches. They were unhappy images, and I felt even worse about them because I wasn't meant to see them. There was the smell of something wet and malted hanging in the air.

"We'll need a fire. It's all there." Jack nodded behind him. "You know how to start one?"

No use in lying, now. "No."

"I don't have staff, you know."

"I know that."

Jack looked at me for the first time. In the eyes, I mean. "You hurt?"

I shook my head. But I also bit my lip. Because I did hurt, quite a lot.

"Wind knocked out of you? Lucky you were on the beach. Would have been a hell of a lot worse on the road. You know what you do if you don't ride?" he asked.

I shook my head, again.

"You don't." Jack walked to the stove. Kneeled down, grabbed a handful of straw and wood bits for the fire.

"Even a child of Leonora's has to know not to ride into a storm. I'm surprised you made it as far as the beach. You put Señor Teyo in danger, you know." He shook his head and stuffed more kindling in the fire. "You struck me as someone who spends at least a fraction of her time thinking of people other than herself. Did I get you wrong?"

"No, sir," I said. "No."

"You've eaten? Of course you haven't. Don't answer that. You wouldn't have gone out on a full stomach. Only someone hungry would have done something so foolish. Rabbit stew is all I got." He put a heavy casserole on the stove. "And some tortillas. Barely drinkable wine. That's the thing I miss the most. Everything here arrives vinegared from the heat. Have some water," he said, dipping a ladle into a pot next to the cookstove. "For your scare."

The glass was warm and I was glad for it. I felt cold right through. I felt that if I were left alone, I'd be shaking like a puppy, born without full fur. My humiliation was the only thing providing any warmth at all.

"And here," Jack said, cracking something from a foil packet on a shelf above the stove. "Chocolate. Your sugar's probably down."

I accepted the chunk gratefully. It had a bitter taste with a bit of heat to it, like eating teeming dirt.

Jack let go a mighty exhale, losing height as he did breath. He got down on his knees again, watching his fire try to go, and I felt the weight of my imposition once again. He was a man not used to having company, and now we had to talk.

"I bet I lose some cows," he said, his tone forced, which I was glad for. It would have been even worse to pass the storm in silence. "You know that they lie down? Bellies east, backs west. Horses do that too. You can tell the coming weather from them, days and days before. But those cows . . . lightning hits and they all get it. You come out in the morning, they're all still lying down. You don't know until you get right up there whether they're scared or dead."

He rose to his feet. The fire had finally started. Jack latched the door on it, and the room lost some of its glow. I looked to his bed, and he saw me.

"Go ahead," he said. "Sit. It's never fun to fall."

I didn't really want to; it made me feel more helpless. There was a table across from his bed, near one of the closed windows, but it had only one chair. Jack sat down in it, and I sat on his bed, because what else was there to do? I watched him take his boots off.

"Leonora know you're gone?"

I shook my head. I hadn't heard my own voice say too many words yet, and it seemed frightening to try.

"Well," he said, his long hands on the table. "She'll know soon enough."

"I doubt that she'll care," I managed, watching the way the fire danced.

"She'll care," Jack said, nodding with me at the flames. "When the others notice."

My heart fell at this. It was true, but I thought he might say something more generous than that.

Jack stood back up, took down an unmarked bottle from the shelf with a yellow splash inside.

"I wouldn't usually offer a young lady tequila," he said, grabbing two tin cups. "But you're shaking. I could give you a shirt." He held the cups a moment, still. "I probably should. They're not entirely clean, though."

"No, no," I said, heating to imagine just what his shirt would smell of. "I'm fine."

"Tequila, then," he said, pouring two cups out, and not too much for me. "Just sip."

I closed my hands around the mug. Knowing he was watching made me shake all the more. I sniffed the liquid first, smelled saddle and old tin. The taste wasn't much better, ghastly and all pucker, like being forced to drink from a washed-out perfume bottle. The color of old chamomile with a whole life inside it.

"Warmer?" he asked.

And I laughed. I couldn't believe I laughed. The sound of it made me realize that the rain had slowed.

"Hear that?" Jack asked, looking toward the ceiling. "That silence? Never good. You know about the oracles? The horse ones?"

"I think so?" I lied.

"Hippomancy. Do you know what I'm saying? My horses have known for days about the storm. And yours too." He shook his head. "So abysmally stupid," he said, still doing the shaking. "I'm almost impressed. But you've heard about it, haven't you? The oracles?" He took some of his tequila. "A horse is running through a pasture, head down, for no apparent reason?" He raised his shoulders in either a shrug or an attempt to warm himself; his body was a stiff body, although he was relaxed. "A neighbor's life will end. Their tails swell, get a shaggy look to them? Rain will come in a few days. The Celts used to leave the question of war to their white horses. A clever, clever folk. They'd draw a line where the battle would commence, and have a white horse cross it. If the horse crossed with his left foot, they'd call the battle off."

I found these stories terrifying. I could see the white horse on the battleground. And the armed men, holding breath.

Jack made as if he were looking out the window. The window that was closed. "War is going to come for our countries," he said. "You're old enough to know that."

I swallowed what I could of the drink he'd given me.

"I'm telling you this because I don't know what slosh Leonora invents. Who plans a museum, now?"

"They wouldn't take the paintings," I offered, the drink making me bold.

"Who wouldn't?"

"The Louvre."

Jack's eyes went huge. "You're serious."

"They said she was peddling trash."

He bellowed. Raised his glass. "What a tremendous compliment!" He actually got up and clinked my glass. "To trash! She's got a good number of mine with all the rest of them. I'm honored." He was smiling to himself. "Rejected by the Louvre. As well we should be! We're not making art of the dead! You're housed up with some of the greatest jackasses of this century, but at least their art's alive."

"So you do like them?" I dared.

"You can hate a man but still respect his art. In fact, I don't think I could tolerate the work of a man I actually liked. Except perhaps for your Walter, there. Although he's a cartoonist. Sardonic lot."

"He isn't well," I said.

"And he shouldn't be. None of us should be. We should be worried and we should be guilty and we should be very scared. But she finds that all beneath her, your mother." He took more of his drink. "Or rather, she's completely insensitive to it. Was built with different fuses. It almost makes you wonder if something's—" He stopped. "I'm sorry. Forgive me. Forgive this kind of talk."

I both wanted to hear more and wanted to hear none of it. I'd heard the talk, of course, that my mother was dim-witted, that senselessness ran in the family, that my own great-grandmother talked only in singsong, that her husband found it preferable to shoot himself than to listen to her warble. Jack continued with the drinking, not really intent on it, not like my mother's loons, but probably it was because I wasn't saying anything back. I didn't know what to. I'd had sips of wine with meals, of course, but nothing like tequila—this brushy, grassy thing pushing thrills through like a snake. I had to pause for the whole of it now that the shame was fading, the madness of the recent hours. A great beach conquered on horseback, and me underneath the starshine with no breath left in my chest. And now, a conversation, with no one to correct me. And no one else to hear.

"May I ask you something?" I tried, more nervous by our silence than the thought my voice might break.

"You may," Jack said, "but I may choose not to answer."

"Charlotte called you Heinrich. From the pool. The other day?"

"Observant. We might just make an artist of you yet."

I did, diary. I glowed.

"Heinrich," he said, getting up to spoon his stew. He tasted it. Spooned it into bowls. "I'm sorry." He handed a thick bowl to me, cradled by a greasy napkin. "I only have this one chair. You'll sit at the table?"

"I'm fine," I said, looking to the left of me. "The fire." I hoped from my expression that he understood I needed the warming.

He watched me for a bit. Because I didn't know what else to do, I ate.

"Heinrich," he started up again, after some stew and more tequila. "It was something we were all doing, after the war." He scratched the back of his neck, uncomfortable, I feared. "My closest friend, Helmut, he became John. And Grosz went George, which I teased him for. George!"

I had no idea why he was laughing, so I laughed a little as well.

"So close, the two, why change? But I liked Jack, the sound of it. Everyone in Germany was trying to turn us against England. But the English loved our art. We were doing things then, this lot of us, a kind of riot we called Dada. Which means—" Jack paused here, and pushed his food around. "Well, it doesn't mean anything," he snorted. "Which was the point of it, you know. 'Controlled hysteria.'" He grinned in his remembering. "The Germans wanted 'inoffensive landscapes.' Put out an edict for it, even, and it became a rule. Changing our names was a way to stand up for what we were making. Or so we thought! And then you go by one name long enough, and that's the name that's yours." He dug back into his food.

I scraped at my own stew, my belly nervous from everything I could ask.

"Is it true you knew the Führer?" I decided on, spoon halfway to my mouth.

"Christ," went Jack. "Of course. A wretched little snivel. But we used to have good fun with him, firing him right up. Helmut used to collage things onto his awful landscapes. He'd put a cutout of a dead cow into one of his fields, or paint figures engaged in, well, let's say 'engaged in their activities' beneath some pretty tree. One time, Schlechty—that's how we called him, it's from the German for a kind of bad—he didn't find it until his critique: there was a toppled wine bottle painted near a forest. Beautiful stuff, actually. A fantastic fool, that Helmut."

Jack smiled at his cup as if this Helmut might have been inside of it, swimming up and out. "We had fun for a while," Jack said. "Beautiful. Then he really did it. Bitter little Schlechty. Declared a ban on modernism in the Reich. You couldn't even do allegories. Bit of a letdown for the medievalists, we joked!" Jack's smile looked awful now. "God knows where he is now, Helmut. Or any of the others. Helmut jumped right out of a balcony when the National Socialists took over. And walked to Czechoslovakia. That's right," he said, catching my expression. "Walked." He looked back in his cup and I wished it all for him. Wished them back, his friends, the funny drawings. "And I ended up in

Costalegre. And it's all starting again." He bit his thumb a bit. Looked over. "I'm sorry." He frowned. "I don't know how to make conversation to . . . with little girls."

I wanted to protest that I was not a little girl, but there were so many ways that he could prove this to the contrary, and if he did, I'd probably cry.

"Shall I ask you something, then?" Jack said.

"Yes?" I braced myself.

"You know that if you don't want to be here, you could say something. You could simply say something. Leonora has been known to change her mind."

"Say what?" I did not appreciate my mother being brought into our evening. "It's not like we can go home."

"What home?" he answered. "It doesn't need to be Europe, but this is no place for a girl."

"She wanted me with her, you know," I said, more loudly than I planned.

"She did," I insisted, when he said nothing in reply. "She took me instead of Stephan. I was . . . she chose me." My voice wavered, so I coughed. "She's not . . . she's not what people say about her. My mother . . . she believes that something could come of it. My art."

I let the sentence hang there. Would it rise or would it fall? Worse yet, it floated, pointless and rejected, out into the dark.

Jack crossed his hands upon his leg. He was thinking through his words now, and that made me feel worse. "Does your brother paint?"

"He could, but no."

"Do you mean he's good?"

"He certainly could be. But it doesn't interest him."

"Clever boy. What does?"

"Oh, sports. Walking up mountains. Skiing down them. And he'll probably go into banking, too, one day."

"I see. Well, someone's got to keep the art boat afloat!"

"Do you really think that it could sink?"

"I think it probably won't," Jack said, sipping his drink, which made me realize I'd stopped noticing the way mine felt. "I don't think it's going to reach us. We can't even get the post. And your mother thinks her collection is going to arrive here safe and sound? She's always thought the best of people, it's charming, in its way. It actually is quite charming. I don't want you to think otherwise. I like your mother very much. I just think she's selfish with you. Tugging you around."

"Well, what should you know about it?" I blurted. "You don't even have any!"

"Any what now?"

"Children!"

"It's true," Jack said, looking amused. "I don't."

"So what do you know?!" I yelled, because he looked

close to laughing, and I couldn't have him laugh.

"Apparently, not much." His voice was different and was closed to me. I'd really done it, then. "I'm sorry," he said, rising. "I'll let you go to bed." He picked up his plate and mug and then reached out for mine.

"I'm not finished."

"There's nothing left."

"I'll ride back, you know!"

"Ha!" He laughed. "Give me your plate, won't you, and the rest of that tequila, I think, too."

"Why don't you have a family?" I insisted, still clutching the plate.

"Ah," Jack said, grabbing my dish and my tequila. "How much of life do you want to know?"

He placed the dishes in a sink and ladled water over them, from a dirty bowl. The sound was a warm clutter, and the storm had further quieted. With the closeness and the silence I felt like we were traveling across the whole of Costalegre in a massive blimp.

"I know a little."

"I had a woman, and she left me for a woman. Did you know that?"

He started drying the plates busily while I tried to tame my face.

"Not that I can blame her," Jack continued, drying. "If I were a woman, I wouldn't want a man either."

"So there you go," he said, after I gave him no reply. "Are you satisfied? Any other questions?"

"Won't you really let me go?" I didn't mean it, which he realized, so this softened him a bit.

"No one's going anywhere," he said, a gentleman again. "We're only in the eye of it, there'll be another storm coming any hour. You sleep here." He indicated the bed by the small stove. "I'll sleep in my studio. There's an outhouse in the back. Make sure it's cleared for snakes first." He laughed. "First thing in the morning, if my horse hasn't been struck by lightning, I'll see you home."

I sat there clasping my hands like a small child, because deprived of my drink and dinner plate, I had nothing else to clasp.

Jack washed the dishes still remaining. Dried them. I didn't offer help.

"You know," I said, suddenly desperate for another chance. "She isn't always terrible."

"Lara," he said, a stopping to his movements. "I know."

If I did art in Jack's style, then I would do the landscapes.

Baldomero's tower would be black and white, a cob over the sea.

The squares of cotton fabric would be hanging inside loops of barbed wire, dried out from the sun.

Maybe it wouldn't be just painting. I could make a hoof-print out of sand and deep inside, a thousand pieces of live jellyfish that would make all of the sand glow.

There'd be drastic weather. A soldier climbing out of snow.

Or the belly of our art boat? From a mermaid's view. Not the belly. Hull.

How much water would it take to make a beached piano move?

Domingo

That night—that one—Jack went into the room beyond the curtain. Later, I thought how it would have been completely dark as he'd left me all the lanterns; he didn't even have the fire. How curious to know that a space is there and being used by someone but not to know the room. I didn't mean to fall asleep, but the rain had slowed, was lulling, and I did.

When I woke, dawn had broken, but the embroidered curtain between our areas was closed. I went out as quietly as I could and headed for the outhouse. Snakes didn't matter as much as my need at that point.

While I was getting myself sorted, I heard yelling from the enclosure. Strong words in Spanish. *Estúpidos* again.

I left the outhouse and walked about a little so that it wouldn't look like I was coming from where I was. The sky had gone pink and there was mist over the scrub. I could see horses up and about, neighing and tossing their heads as they ran in circles, then settling with a smugness to push their noses through the grass. Cows too, dark shadows to the corner. And I could see Jack in the middle of this, swinging a lead line at the animals who didn't go where he desired.

I scurried back into the house. Made my little bed. I looked behind me—it was hard to gauge how long Jack would be out there, but I thought I'd hear the gate close when he was done. I decided to look behind the curtain that had separated our beds.

What I saw was a studio, a kind of greenhouse studio: great slabs of stone in the center and blocks and blocks of wood. He was making sculptures from them, but not the forms I knew. They didn't seem to represent anything obvious, circles and huge cubes.

And next to all of this on a table, a wooden block with a figure leaping up and out. Smoothed and arched, this figure, like a bird but without any of the bird things: no feathers and no beak, not even the shape of wings. What it made me think of was the moment right before a heron flies. Such odd creatures, "prehistoric" is what Papa used to say. There were a few of them in England; I thought of them as mine. You had to walk quietly, or else they'd fly away. But still, that moment just before they went, it was like that, it was slow, like they might decide to stay.

I was doing something that I shouldn't have been, but the shapes made me feel calm. In all the places mother's forced me, I'd never seen such stillness, or such gigantic stones. Plus there is something so old and wise about it, about the wood, and stone.

Behind the leaping figure and the other carvings there were two more sections of the studio, one immaculate and empty, the second cluttered with wooden tree trunks and stone objects placed here and there. A faceless head on a gray block. An egg the size of a boulder. Pulleys hanging from the ceiling and a broken chandelier. A wooden trough filled with chisels and an axe.

This was where the smell had come from. The smell of stone being chipped into something else. There was a saddle blanket on a stone slab where Jack must have spent the night. I had known so many of my mother's artists but I'd never known a sculptor. I stared at the immensity of things that were and weren't.

"Tea?"

I swung around. And burned.

"I'm sorry. I didn't know if—"

"You knew," Jack said, reaching past me to tug the curtain closed. "I saw you zigzagging outside."

I didn't bother trying. "I thought . . . I didn't know. I thought you were a painter?"

"Try getting paints out in this hellscape. The sculpting passes time."

"But everyone said . . ." I stumbled. He was standing close, and I had that feeling, or the knowledge, really, that the storm had stopped, so there wasn't any reason for me to be there anymore. "Everyone said that you weren't working."

"Different kind of work."

He turned, and I stole one more look through the curtain's decorative holes.

"They're so . . . beautiful," I said, not knowing what I wanted to ask exactly. "Is it . . . very hard?"

"It is." Jack busied himself at the woodstove, which was burning low because I hadn't had the intelligence to stuff more wood inside. "It's impossible. And therein lies the sense. Tea? Costs me a fortune to get tea here so let's not drink too much."

"Oh, no. I'm fine."

"I'm joking. Sort of. One has to maintain some sense of decorum. I breakfast like a gentleman. I try."

"I'm very sorry," I said, turning toward his studio, "for where you had to sleep."

"Don't be. It allowed me to feel gallant. Let's get the water going. So. You've seen my sculptures. Going to tell the others what I'm up to?"

"I won't." And of course, I meant it. I am good at holding lies.

"They'll ask."

"I'll tell them what you'd like."

"It's not worth the bother," he said after a silence. "It takes oxen to move them, and I'm not going through that

again. They'll live out their lives here, giant and unseen."
Jack laughed, pleased with his own words. "The most
Dada work I've ever done."

"I really think they're beautiful." This sounded foolish;
it wasn't all of what I felt. What I'd seen in Paris, in the
cities, back at Occidente, it was all so loud and garish, it
conjured only the horrid bits of life. But the smoothness of
his sculptures, all circles, no hard corners, they stilled
something inside of me. They were peaceful. I thought
that they held joy.

"They're pure," I said, embarrassed by the simple word.

But he nodded. "That's the goal I had in mind, so you
have complimented me well."

He poured tea into the same mugs from before. "I do
think it's better if you assure them I'm a cowhand."

The mug burned against my palm now; the tin was far
too hot.

He put it another way: "I work best when people think
that I'm not working."

"But may I come back?" I'd asked this before I'd even
thought it. My face, as you can imagine, went immediately
to red.

"My poor girl, what for?"

"To see what they become?"

This question did something to his face. I don't know
how to describe it. It was like when father would come

downstairs in the stone house, having fixed something in his writing that he'd been twisted with for days. By the next day, it would be gone, but we could tell from his lighter weight on the stair steps, the shining in his eyes, that for a little while, everything would be radiant, and possible, and absolutely fine.

<u>Favorite memories:</u>

I've only seen a picture of it, but I am a small baby, and I am being held, and there is me and Papa and Stephan and Mumma laughing beautifully, and the house—there were so many—the house completely white.

<u>Fun words:</u>

la papelería: paper shop
la bufanda: scarf

Domingo—the same one

On our ride back to Occidente, the sky was blue, and except for the branches here and there across the pathway (several of which I jumped!), nature had put the storm behind her. The air smelled clean and fresh, not dank and hanging as it usually does. The world smelled quite alive.

Along the way, I indulged the sight that we would make, me and "Heinrich" Klinger trotting up the entrance path. Hetty would swoon, I knew it, and even Mumma would be impressed. She'd run for me, make a show about it, maybe even cry. I'd be held to various breasts and patted. Relief. Relief for all!

The house was in a state when we arrived. A bamboo dining chair was in the driveway. Fronds marring the way, gone yellow at the tips. A figure ran across an upstairs patio. A female voice yelled from the far side of the house. I felt that something I had lost had finally been restored.

To have Jack see the state I'd caused. You see! I thought. I'm missed!

I worried with the hullabaloo that our approach might not be heard, but Mumma came running out in one of her sack dresses from Africa, the ones she dons when she doesn't know what she wants to dress in yet. She had an aviator hat on but her face wasn't made up. It had been ages since I'd seen her lips so pale.

"Oh heavens!" she cried, running toward us, which made the horses start. "You heard! How wonderful! You'll help!"

"Good morning to you, too, madam," Jack said, shortening his reins.

"The two of you, how charming! Lara, don't you look fetching on that horse! Have I made them nervous? Oh God, I'm so relieved!" She fell upon me, one hand on the horse's neck, her cheek against my leg. I resisted the urge to run my hand along her little hat.

"Eduardito!" she hollered, raising her head with effort. "Eduardo! We'll get your horse some water, then we can head back out? Finally, relief! Here, here, let me hold your horse, Jack. Or try! Eduardo will come out any moment; you'll have something to eat. Let's see if I can handle the both of them—Lara, yours is a little—ah, there you go, how marvelous! You do still ride so well! And the pink in your cheeks! Isn't she just lovely! If only there were time to enjoy such a thing! Jack, darling, do you still have a way with tracks? Our thinking is behind us here at the start of that horrid forest. What sort of thing should I wear to look for him? I imagine all manner of thorns."

"Leonora," Jack said, looking down at her, "could you make even the slightest effort to make sense? I prefer my discourses middling at this early hour."

"But Baldomero's <u>gone</u>!" she cried. "Taken with the storm! He could be any of the places! There's no way to know! It's just horrid. It's just horrible. What if he's really gone!"

"Leonora—"

"He went out for his monkey! On his monkey search! He brought Caspar, certainly. This was before lunch yesterday. And you do know that Baldomero never misses lunch! Oh God! It's been nearly a day!" She pressed her head against my calf and my heart recoiled. I should have stayed on that wet beach. Let the vultures come.

"Leonora, for God's sake, I've brought your daughter back!"

"And it was so kind of her to fetch you! You're the only one who knows—"

"Mother!" I shouted. And then I undid all the good that Jack might have tried to think of me. I dismounted. Badly. And ran into the house.

<u>Stupid words:</u>

useless

maybe

Stephan

ARTIST

the jungle should take ME!

This is what the sculpture looked like that I saw jumping wood.

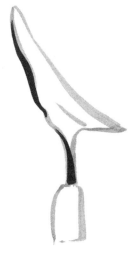

Tonight while I lay in bed waiting for the voices I considered that it could be a porpoise as much as it could be: bird.

Domingo—NOCHE!

Tell me if there is anything worse, anything more horrible, than a total inability to plot things. All of these incompetencies show that I can't ride off on my own. I don't speak Spanish, I don't know where to go. And anywhere I <u>could</u> go, I'd need mother to pay. I don't have the first idea of how you find a means of transportation in this horrid country, and father and Stephan are leagues across the ocean, and war is coming for them, and there is absolutely not a place, not a single place where it would be safe for me to go!

It is horrible to be a young girl and to know little more than what? How to paint a picture?! And it's not even worth <u>drowning</u> myself because mother wouldn't even note it! I hate everything about this! I hate this stupid world!

And nowhere even to cry in! I fled to my room and moved the mattress in front of the door, that stupid, stupid curtain blowing back and forth and getting caught on my round mattress. I can't even have a door! The sun deck's all I have for privacy, the little jot that I don't know what to do with because it's burning hot. If I could speak the language here, I could call for a boat. But what kind of boat? To where? And I can't travel alone, not really. What a curse to be a girl!

So I went out on the balcony sniveling and burning, the sun impossible for eyes. If I jumped onto the ground below, would anyone note that? Really, the ocean's the only way because at least I know I'd drown, having never been taught a single useful thing in this whole world!

For a while after, I could hear everyone calling out below. Not for me: just out. Mother and Jack fighting, or him fighting with someone else. You know, I can't trust him either. I will let you know I want to. But I am not a child, even if he would like to make mother think I am. There have been people before, before him. Who thought of me, but better. C. for example, who breaks my mother's heart with her hard talent and her body. I think sometimes she tried, or at least I thought I felt her trying, but in the end, it's always shock and nakedness and angry, closed, shut doors. No one in this world cares about anyone but themselves, especially not these artists, the most famous, the most stupid, the worst in all the world.

And I know <u>Elisabeth</u> isn't living a misery like mine, wherever she is. I should be an orphan; at least I'd be in school! At least people would make sure that I was in bed at night, at the least, that! Instead of this, which is never-ending nothingness, nowhere for me to be. If I had a door I would throw myself upon my bed and weep and keep it locked for decades. Birds could come and drop me bits of fish from the blue sea. I'd ride away on a great bird. Or I'd be a cliff diver like the ones we saw the last time we were out here—what a thing to be. I'm always alone and I'm never alone, and there is nothing I can do!

I hope that ship sinks, I hope it burns, that's the only thing there is. If it were here now I'd set fire to it, I'd throw the paintings in the sea. I'd sink her awful collection, and then what would she do? There'd be nothing left to fawn over and boast about and move around the world for and maybe she would be emptied enough to finally mother me.

Popocatépetl and the Sleeping Woman

In another legend that Magda used to tell me, a great warrior fell in love with a beautiful young girl. Popocatépetl was the warrior and Iztaccíhuatl, the princess. They lived in the valley of the pueblo and the air was full of flowers.

But one day, their neighbors to the south decided to wage some war on them. Popocat had to go, because he was a warrior, and Izta understood this. They agreed to marry upon his return.

But there was another warrior in their village who was jealous of their love. When the southern battle was in fact going quite well for the brave warriors, the jealous one sent back a false message to Izta that her Popocat had died.

Despite her father's love for her and the villagers' concern, Izta stopped eating and drinking and died of a sad heart.

When Popocat returned victorious to his village and heard of his love's loss, he asked the villagers to help him build a funeral table for Izta high up in the hills. He laid down Iztaccíhuatl and covered her with a cloak, and then

Popocatépetl sat beside her with a great and smoking torch, determined to watch over her in her forever sleep.

Years passed. Then centuries. Popocat watched over Izta so long that he died himself, and the snow covered them, and the hillsides grew and grew until each of their sorrowful bodies turned into its own mountain: Izta's flat and sleeping, Popocat's rounded and watching over her.

Magda had seen these mountains, and said that every once in a great while, Popocat's mountain starts to burn and smoke with rage. It trembles and it sputters and it makes the entire valley shake, and that is how you know that Popocat is still furious with grief.

From the preface to "Mexican Plants for American Gardens," 1935

To satisfy this demand for new and interesting plant material, renowned plantsmen have explored the far reaches of the earth. But, strange to say, in all the searchings for new and rare material, plant hunters have barely touched the floral treasures of the vast North American continent. It is only within recent years that gardeners have become aware of the really worthwhile plants.

What day? ¿Qué dia?

Nothing to say and what am I to paint. I thought that he would come for me and of course he hasn't.

Come for me for what?

I had hopes for Stephan and once I had Elisabeth and now I don't know what to want.

Watching over someone after they're already dead is more than loyal, it's romantic. If they're dead, that is true love. The only other romantic thing is something Hetty told me on one of the nights when she felt powerful. Or spiteful, is the word. That after the Vienna business, when Mum first came to Costalegre, they all came down for breakfast at the pink casita and there was a horse inside the house. That the horse had on a bright blanket with pink and green run through it and flowers in its mane, and a man in white holding on to it so it wouldn't run. Konrad had bought a horse for C. so that she could ride.

What happened to it? What happened to the horse?

"I don't know," said Hetty, lolling. "I think that it was sold."

Dear Stephan,

Papa will be pleased to know that Baldomero's three days gone. At first, it was suggested as an act of cunning. That perhaps he had gone missing to drive his prices up, but no one is going to buy paintings if there's a war, so that makes little sense.

Mother rounded everybody up, even the grooms from the main stable. We all spread out at different distances, although I walked with Hetty because (I didn't write you about this!), I had recently been somewhat lost myself, and everyone was frantic, of course, to keep me from going missing yet again. So we all walked straight as possible, the idea being that one of us, eventually, would find them. (Caspar had gone out with Baldomero on the day they disappeared, Baldo terribly eager to find a monkey pet. In point of fact, I've learned from Hetty that kinkajous aren't even monkeys, they're actually small bears, but I don't suppose it makes a difference because neither of them was found.)

The general suspicion is that Baldomero disappeared himself, subscribed to by most here except for Walter and mother and Hetty, who are convinced that he's been kidnapped, and that they'll soon come for the rest of us as well. Walter thinks it's the Germans, but you know he hasn't been well. I do think mother's right in saying that the Germans are deeply occupied with other matters at this instant, and no one knows exactly where we are. I mean, you do. But there is a difference between knowing and trying to get here!

I don't know what I think. To be honest, I think Baldomero was quite fond of Costalegre, and he certainly doesn't know how to do anything by himself. I do think that it's possible that Caspar did something terrible. No one is really well. It's the not knowing, and the heat here, and the light is always the same. There is something chilling about there being too much sun.

Maybe he sold Baldomero to someone? It would serve Baldomero right, he's been awful to everyone that works here and everyone in the house. Or maybe they did find that little bear, except it wasn't little. I've only seen a few of them but there are, apparently, all manner of creatures in the jungle, including those sorceresses with backward-facing feet—do you remember when Magda told us those dark tales? You cried once, listening to her, although I bet you won't remember it that way.

In any case, there is an elevated air of care and of concern. And for once, people are working less and being kind. Would you believe, for example, that I planted something with our Mumma? Seeds for lemon trees, in fact. And it was Mum who came up with the idea; I don't know if you can plant a lemon tree using only lemon seeds, but that is what we did, and not even by the poolside. In a more private place, so they would be our private trees. It was really her idea.

I've been painting a lot, also, using odder colors because we're low on paint. Ferdinand has found a berry that you can crush into a colored dust. It's hard to work with, but we have the time. I will probably go out and pick more with him, and we'll identify some others. There are colors from the seeds and things that you can't get with any of the paints the artists have, so really, it's quite special. I think it would be nice to bring them into my drawings: that is, most of the picture would be paper and charcoal, and then you'd have this splash of something, berry paint.

In any case, the house has been easier with Baldomero gone. Maria, the cook here, is absolutely joyful. I think he was the worst with her. All through the day, she's singing songs again. Really, it's quite joyful, and if you get this (I'm going to try to get mother to ask Jose Luis about it properly, this time), you should consider this not as an invitation, but as us imploring: I think that you should come! Surely by this time of year you could use the change of climate? And we haven't had news about it, but who knows what's happening with the war by now. I'm sure it's much gayer and lighter here than Europe. Still no news of Mumma's boat!

Yours ever,
(and give my love to Papa)
Lara

Miércoles

The dream briefs continue. I tell the (almost) truth because I'm proud. I know that far away from them, Jack's still making silent shapes. They think they are the artists, but I know what others don't.

I tell Legrand that I dreamt of a studio filled with wood and limestone. That I could feel the charred chisel in my hand. The gold and tilting porpoise shape, up, up, and away. I draw a golden creature darting through the sea, all smoothness and possibility, as light as the comb jellies Jack showed me, the predators behind. But the porpoise is never caught because he can thrust himself away from them, high and long above the water, it is as if he flies.

Legrand was very moved to hear that my dolphin had no fins. "You are getting closer to the truth of this," he said.

Viernes

Baldomero and Caspar six days gone now. Mum has sent Jose Luis to Zapata over and over, and he'll leave for Vallarta soon to put a word in with the embassy. Legrand laughed about this, saying the Spanish rebels weren't going to want a surrealist back during a civil war.

Ferdinand has started piling rocks outside his bedroom curtain. An idea I hadn't thought of.

Domingo

C. is discontented. She has finished a first draft of her manuscript and she wants to go to Puerto Vallarta to have it typed. She wants to go herself. She doesn't trust someone else taking all her pages. But she will need a few days in Vallarta and Jose Luis can't escort her, Mum needs him here at Costalegre, so the situation can't be resolved. She wants her novel on heavier paper, she says. It keeps blowing around.

She's started up her walks again, so I go when she'll have me, and I try to talk of other things but she isn't a foolish person and so we talk of Jack. She knows now where I was that night; everyone agrees that it was gallant and unlike him. People asked what I saw inside his home and I said I couldn't say. That there was a closed room. That I saw only sketchbooks.

I asked C. about the sketchbooks. I said I saw more than I did so she would talk as if I knew things, and then it was just a matter of stretching my mind to imagine what else I might have seen.

"You probably saw the old ones," she said, her voice tired. It's true that with Legrand insisting so much on it, we haven't been getting enough sleep. "The ones he did at war. You wouldn't have believed it, though, what he started out with. This was before everything, before I even knew him, his work was realistic. You know, almost pastoral, as the Führer wanted."

She kicked a rock out of the way with her soft boot.

"They recruited people. To paint the Central Powers. Germany and Austria-Hungary, all of their fine boys. But they get there, all these artists, and they're told they can't paint bodies. That they must paint 'courage.' That they must paint 'will.'

"So Heinrich started doing trees," she said. "Trees like burning bodies. When he came back from the front, they couldn't share the paintings. The German government. They were just too ghastly. So that's one of the things that got him into trouble."

Now I wanted to go through them. Go through all the paintings. My heart sprung to imagine that I had seen only the slightest bit of everything Jack had done. Even if it's true that they have seen things, Mum's loonies are so peevish, it's hard to believe that they have been through something bad. With Jack, though, it is different. In this, he's like Konrad. If there's pain, he doesn't talk.

"He wasn't the only one discharged," C. said, kicking at a twig. "Most of the paintings were confiscated, his and the other war artists'. They were probably burned. Maybe that's what broke him, in the end."

"Broke him, how?"

She looked at me as if my naiveté were taking up all the space between us.

"He doesn't believe in it anymore. The art making."

"I don't think that's true," I said, without thinking first.

C. closed her lips together.

"He cares for you, how funny," she said, plucking a closed bud from a tree.

Martes

Normally I just do scenes inside of houses. But I'm trying the outside. The lemons that the small goat cast down from the tree, and his blood on the white ground. The Montezuma cypress on the polo field that the horses gallop round. The outside of Jack's cabin, with a sunset that's half storm. I am thinking of the things inside his sketchbook that I didn't see.

I am also painting because Jack hasn't come. I imagine he is working with his sculptures, divining the weather from his horses' tails. I'm sure if I actually tried to go back there, everything would be ruined. He heard me ask if I could come but he didn't say I could. There is just so much in silence. If I don't go back I can make Jack Klinger be anything at all.

Dear Lara,

I have found Magda for you. You'll start lessons in the morning.

Dear Lara,

I have reached your father. He is safe but he's regretful. Konrad has to go to the museum and your brother's coming back.

Lara, love,

I would put bright flowers, also, around a mane, a horse.

Lara,

I know your mother means well because she told me that it's true.

Lara,

I have seen the art boat. It will be there, soon.

Lara,

How embarrassing to lack even the imagination for the proper words! I will tell you what you'll always be and it's inconsequential!

Potos
flavus   kinkajou

POTOS FLAVUS

According to another book of Hetty's, kinkajous have
long prehensile tails that they can climb up if the other
end of the tail is stabilized. They sleep all day and wake
just as the parents are trying to put their children to night.

Jueves

Not exactly a confirmation, but money was given to a
dock porter in Puerto Vallarta who said that a man fit-
ting Caspar's description had boarded the SS Mexican
for a one-way trip to California. It was mother who gave
the money, and Jose Luis who went to the dock. No pas-
sengers with capes or queer mustaches or monkeys on
their arms, is the information he came back with. Konrad
said that Baldomero probably went disguised as Caspar,
and mother protested that she'd rarely seen Baldo as
inspired as he'd been here, to which new father answered,
"Your impressions are your own."

Baldomero loves subterfuge. Baldomero loves disguises.

"But he left all his canvases behind," said mother, "even
his favorite comb."

No one wants to think about what this means, but I
think of it at night.

A bird flew in my window yesterday and died, even
though there isn't glass.

Calaway Jeune

(Calaway, très jeune!)

Season Opener, Christmas ? : Children's Art!!

*Principal: Little Lucian's drawings, showing such great prom-
ise and the Sigmund link will make them flock!*

*Secondary: That handsome South African's daughter—Tessa?
Anna? The poet fellow. Wife?*

Tertiary: ? Surely Legrand knows a lovely child.

*Necessary: Lara's. The ones of the women milking are actually
quite good.*

Calaway—New York?

Sábado

I think that mother should be more <u>judicious</u> with her notes!

Lucian Freud was my classmate when I was still allowed to be in classes and I will have you know he took a cat's eye out with a pebble once!

And Anna Campbell is only interesting to mother because of her nice accent and her handsome father who is a COMMUNIST, I'll add, and in another life—in another great one—my paintings will be quite necessary indeed.

Day?

I am just intelligent enough to realize that Jack hasn't asked after me, and if there is one thing I've learned from watching mother it is that when you're not wanted, you're not asked.

I dream of him sculpting, regardless, and it shouldn't be exciting (I've seen sculptures), but it is. He doesn't care about us and it makes mother infuriated, but I am going to allow myself to believe he cares for me. What else is there to do.

In any case, it feels enough to paint for him. I'm sure that's what he'd want. He definitely seems like a person who values artists working, instead of artists putting papaya mush on their nipples and throwing the maid's bell in the pool. In any case, even if I wanted to be fool-hardy (which I do not), Hetty has established a system wherein you have to ask her for permission each time you leave the house.

So even if I tried to go to Jack's again (which I will not), Hetty would insist on going with me, and if she did, she'd see his work, and even though he acted as if he wouldn't care if the others knew that he was sculpting, I think that he would.

When you are making something beautiful, you must be left alone. This is a posture mother thinks is rubbish but Konrad and C. don't. Do you know, my diary, that Mum wanted school also? She has told me on the wine nights how terribly she wanted friends. I also know that mother gives Hetty 850 francs a month. She tells me things and she forgets that she has told me, and when I remind her of the worst things, she says I'm a "terrible delight."

I have known chaos, but I've never known this chaos. Maria refuses to return to Occidente because she found a "Mariposa de la Muerte" in the kitchen, and mother lost her patience and said if Maria was so frightened of moths, perhaps Maria should clean better, and without Baldomero, there wasn't anyone to understand the Spanish she talked back. C. speaks a little, but she's in a trance about her book.

Regardless though, I have that light feeling, even with the mess. I feel calm and little and a little bit delighted, like very soon someone is going to show me what I need to do. In the meantime, I paint and I draw and I think I am improving. I think about the sculptures I saw in Jack's glowing room, the leaning creature fleeing its own wood.

The malted bits of stone discarded and the place where "Heinrich" slept.

Even though nothing ever gets here in the way it should, I think that maybe one day, when I am far away and schooling somewhere pleasant, that I can write Jack letters or maybe send him drawings—he needn't ever respond. Wouldn't that be something, Jack under his roof here confronting my improvement, while I'm wherever I have gone.

Plus, I have a secret, and sometimes (depending on the secret) secrets make me calm. I also saw the moth. My diary: he was beautiful, with a face on the back of his big body, brown and yellow like a tiny monkey head. I feel he chose Maria and he also chose my room, and I like to imagine that he has gone to Jack now, and said, "It is time to save them," and that it will only be a matter of some evenings until there is an actual real car, or maybe a boat and then a car, and then I will have some of my things back because it must be clear now even to my mother that you can't have a museum in a country where mountain lions howl.

Sábado

Walter is missing, also. And also, Ferdinand. The curtain blows into his bedroom and there isn't anyone inside.

Hetty is in hysterics. Walter left all of his forging equipment and he can't get back without it. Mother says of course he can, he already got everyone here and how much equipment do you need, really, to do cartoons? I don't know how she thinks it all a joke. This is something that Papa was always yelling at her, you think it all so funny. But then he would be delighted by the way she saw things; it depended on his mood. He said the back of language broke on mother, that she was impossible to talk to. He said that she was moved by everything and truly moved at nothing. At dinner last night, Konrad told Hetty that my mother wasn't intelligent enough to experience fear, that it was like cohabitating with a bovine, and mother said he'd lost his sense of humor in the internment camp.

"What to think of it?" she answered, when Konrad had left the table, too tired to fight. She said that she could be paranoid, or she could be disinterested, and that neither attitude was bringing her any news about her boat, so if she chose to be amused by the fact that her guests found life in the jungle preferable to her company, so be it.

"But Leonora," Hetty said, "what if they come for us? What if they come for Lara?"

"Even savages can be reasonable," she answered. "There's little that can't be negotiated over good food and clean wine."

"But the wine here is terrible," muttered Legrand.

"My dear ungrateful comrade." Mother smiled. "Perhaps you will go next."

~~My~~ <u>Chère</u> <u>diary</u>:

Nothing to do so I will tell you something else. The day I returned to Occidente with Jack, they did send out a search party. It of course became a real one, a real party like they do. I painted and I painted, making pouts up in my tower, but nicely, because I was sure that Jack would come to check on me and would see the things that I was painting and he would understand.

He did not come. Hours passed. I felt like screaming for it—was I truly so uninteresting that I didn't make anyone curious?? I could have let the night come but I don't think I would have survived it. So I took one of my new drawings, not the ones that Mum finds so naive. This was a scene under the ocean: jelly combs and anemones playing a type of house. It was really drawn quite nicely and a little strangely, and "strange" usually means best. Anyway, I took it and I made my way outside without anybody seeing me and I put it in the satchel that was attached to Jack's fine horse. My heart was beating mightily and everything was lit up by the lanterns, and the sound of the artists laughing was both distant and quite happy; there was a calm again, you know.

On my way back upstairs I steeled my courage and went by the palapa to bid everyone good night, which is not something that I do usually, which my mother pointed out. Jack did look at me when I said it—you know, in that way that feels like something has been thrown directly toward you, as if you're on the other end of a straight line. Back in my room, I waited. For some kind of . . . knotting. I fell asleep, eventually. At one point, there was someone. In the doorway. But it was someone else.

Sábado, still Sábado

Once upon a time there was a giant who put down a cement copa for the other gods to drink from, and they did drink, until there was no water in the sea.

Once upon a time there was a heartsick woman who drowned her children in a river to scorn the man who had left her, and this didn't make him return to her, and all her children were dead.

On one of C.'s horse rides, she saw a rock formation that proves that Ferdinand is still here. But I've seen those rocks before. I saw them the other times I had to go to Teopa by myself, each of them pushed carefully into a certain plot of sand.

I don't think he's hiding.

The stories for the children are the saddest ones of all.

Lunes

We went back for Jack that day, the day after C. had gone out looking for Ferdinand because she'd seen the rocks. I finally told her that I'd already seen them well before he disappeared, and since she had put a lot of emotion into the proof of those formations, she decided that Ferdinand must be really gone or drowned, or in one of the caves here, and that Jack knows the tides well, so we could rely on him to pick the right times to go into the caves.

I am going to tell you something. C. asked me to come. I really think that she is sensitive, and that there is a part of her that understands. She didn't even make it a question, she said, "We'll go for Jack," and diary, I felt very much the lady and even rode my horse well, so pleased was I at the thought of where we were going and to have somewhere to go.

Jack's house was clean and very tidy; you forget how tidy something can be when you live with people who aren't.

The branches that had fallen had been stacked and burned. I can understand the tidy symmetry of a life lived all alone.

It isn't that I want to live with him. I want to write that. Because I know that I'm not helpful. Not in the important ways, and I'll never be strong. It's just that there is something about Jack that makes me feel that I can be still for a while. That he will tell me something and it will be true, that he will continue to live in his small house day after sunny day, taking care of the animals and hacking into stone and wood and listening to people. I don't think I have ever been contemplated. Or maybe I mean considered. Not even by my brother, who prefers a jaunty rope tow to writing me a letter. I'm just Leonora's daughter, the one that has to go places, the more attractive child. The idea that someone thinks of me in private, thinks of how I could be happiest, fills me with both a name-day kind of excitement and a giant grayness. Because they're never as good as you hope they'll be, birthdays.

Lunes, later

We had tea and C. went through Jack's notebooks. They talked in the way of people who know things about each other and I won't write of that.

Jack did not let C. talk as long as she expected to, however. Do you see. Do you see he noticed that I had been quiet for some time.

Maybe one day my horrid mother will find my diary and tell Legrand and everyone that I am *amoureuse*. The surrealists think that passion is important, that nightmares are important. But they don't value simplicity, which is how I think of love. This patient, tense, and quiet thing that is leaving someone alone.

Did I mention that the woman's name is La Llorona and that she takes other people's children to replace the ones she ended, but then she drowns them, too?

Isn't it interesting. How much the loonies value children. But then it's only mother who has any children at all.

Miércoles—I think

Delighted by the missing, Legrand has picked up work
on his Surrealist Manifesto again:

Possibility is a torture that tortures not the dreaming man.
You go where the mind says to. Fire cares not for delay!
Singe what you don't love, love what you will take.
Everything is available, all paths at the same time. Your
essence is inevitable, as are its desires.

. . .

He has probably killed the others. Killed them with my
mother. It wouldn't be impossible, especially because he
believes that nothing is.

Martes

Another thing. The other night at dinner, Legrand announced that he had urges for a painting. Something classical, a nude. "Of Flossy," he joked, and we were eating shrimp. Legrand chews his with their skin on, by the way.

Day?

I've been trying to pretend about it, but there's no use in it, especially as we'll soon go. Jack did get the drawing that I left him in his saddlebag. I asked him by the cave when we went to look for Ferdinand. ~~C. had gone inside with the turtle man who had come to help, and I'm afraid of cl~~

We were waiting for the turtle man, whom Jack had asked to help us, and C. was looking for a better place to tie the horses because even at the cliffs along Teopa, there isn't any shade.

Jack didn't say anything even though we were alone. And I felt sick for that. When people don't say anything, it's because they have something to say. To be truthful, I thought C. would come back and we'd still be in silence. And then he said the truth.

"I found your painting, Lara."

"Oh?" I said, as if it had gone there by itself.

"I'm going to tell you something," he said, and normally someone would pick at a burr or something, but he looked me in the eyes.

"You are good at drawing, but you might not be an artist. You know with Leonora . . . you would have to be the best."

My throat was nearly flaming from my effort not to cry. What kind of person speaks like this, with no softness round their meaning? If C. hadn't been too close for it, I think I would have screamed. Let me tell you what it is like to respond to something hideous when there is nothing you can say.

"Just let it be a pleasure. Let it be a special thing, make everything you want. But don't make it for her."

"I put it there for you," I said too quickly, and of course I turned the color of the fruit names I have learned. "I thought you were a gentleman."

"I've never been accused of such a thing," is what he answered. "Lara, you have promise. You have the soul for it, the heart for it. But you're painting for your mother."

"I most certainly am not."

"Listen." He had his elbows on his knees now. "Have you ever tried to write?"

"I think I'll just help Charlotte, actually," I said, standing up.

And then he touched my hand. Or took it, I don't know, it was a suddenness, like finding something in your bed when your arm goes out in sleep. Like something you might dream, is what I'm saying. Like something wonderful that has happened that you need to keep with you while you're awake. And it was that line again, him on one end. And me on the other. And then it was done and my hand was alone again and C. was coming back.

"Lara," he said, and my name was many openings. My eyes completely filled. "You have to leave."

"Well aren't you just a help," I snapped, unable to look back at him. His insistence that we leave when I wanted to hear the opposite had me furious and who knew where was Ferdinand and the sun was very strong.

"Mother won't, you know," I continued, ashamed because he didn't say anything and my voice had been too loud. "Not without her boat."

"That boat," Jack said, "is not going to arrive."

"And where would you have us go then?" I asked, turning around.

"You could go to California."

Well, isn't it stupid to wish things? Isn't the worst thing to have hope? Isn't the worst thing to be someone who cries in front of people when she is already fifteen long years old?

"But don't you find me interesting?" I blurted, like a fool.

"Maybe I care enough about you to not ruin your life."

And what, diary, what should I make of that? I have let him matter. I can go on to California and pretend I matter back but you understand, of course, that none of it will matter because I have become fond of the one artist that my mother doesn't control.

Precious little flower feather. Stupid bird in space. I was made fragile and most people like to see if I can break.

Can you love someone by making them feel that they are hated? Of course you can. My mother's sister pushed all three of her children off a rooftop but she won't tell you that. Is it even true? Papa would yell and yell that on the awful evenings: "Is it even true, L'nora, is it even true." It's the one thing Mum won't talk of. So you know it's true.

I wish I were a mermaid. I wish that I could swim. I wish that I could scream until my pores were tentacles and I pulled each and every person down with me until life was soft again. And then I would come up on the shore and I'd be human. And I'd know where to go.

Note from the author

While imagining a cover for this book, well-intentioned purists noted that there aren't—that there were never—tigers in Mexico. *Costalegre* is a book where fact and fiction tussle. There are a lot of tigers in this Mexico.

The beginning of the Second World War is the historical backdrop for this novel, which is populated by fictional characters inspired by their real-life artist counterparts, some of whom would actually have been alive and working in 1937, others of whom would have not.

I researched maniacally for this project, until some of the experiences I read about became part of my own makeup. It is a testament to the personality of the American art collector Peggy Guggenheim and the artists she supported that so many of them felt moved to document their time creating—and promoting—art under her protection, which is how I spent a fascinating year in the remembrances of writers such as Leonora Carrington,

Djuna Barnes, André Breton, and Peggy Guggenheim, herself, searching for information about what life was like for Peggy's late daughter, Pegeen Vail Guggenheim.

The names of almost all the artists in this book have been changed: Ferdinand Cheval's has not. His rock palace really does exist in Hauterives, France, and the accompanying plaque that is translated into English on page 20 does, too: *En créant ce rocher, j'ai voulu prouver ce que peut la volonté.*

The real-life Peggy Guggenheim tolerated her various husbands' and lovers' infatuations with other artists in their social circle. So it was that she woke up in the middle of a cocktail party one evening in 1932 (having fallen asleep because the conversation bored her), to find her favored paramour, the notoriously unproductive British writer John Ferrar Holms, fiddling lasciviously with Djuna Barnes's recently washed hair. In her memoir, *Out of This Century*, Peggy proudly recounts how she admonished John for his flirtation: "If you rise, the dollar will fall," a priceless quip that is reproduced on page 36.

The high-profile female artists of this period worked hard to have a profile: they were bawdy, provocative, and wildly inventive in both their art and words. But fighting for their financial and creative independence did not always mean that they were equally generous in the art of sisterhood. Another retort that reflects the slippery stakes of friendship between female artists at this time appears on page 51, when C. applauds Hetty for being "such marvelous company when you're ill!" This is based on something Peggy Guggenheim recalls Djuna Barnes saying to the aspiring writer and compulsive diary keeper Emily Coleman, whom Hetty's character is based on: "You would be marvelous company slightly stunned."

The book *Mexican Plants for American Gardens* by the American geographer and botanist Cecile Hulse Matschat was a 1935 doorstop of a book I found in a Canadian bookshop in the Mexican sea town of Melaque. All of the sections cited in this peculiar book appear as they existed in the 1935 publication except for the chapter on the sandbox tree on page 101, which I wrote. I was desperate for something "extra" for the novel that I was researching while in Mexico, something from the time period that could help my privileged but undereducated fifteen-year-old narrator understand the environment and landscape she suddenly found herself trapped in, and thanks to serendipity and the intrepidness of Cecile Matschat, I found it. Or rather, it found me.

On page 138, the character Konrad completes a dream brief which is based on a mural that the German artist Max Ernst completed in the home of the French poet Paul Éluard in the 1920s, taking its title from one of Éluard's poems, "At the first clear word." "The first youth is closed" is a rough translation of a French line from this particular poem that much inspired Ernst: *la première jeunesse close.*

On page 147, the character called "Papa" is remembered quoting, or rather *mis*quoting, his favorite poet, William Blake. The correct quote is from Blake's 1803 poem "The Mental Traveller":

> *Who nails him down upon a rock,*
> *Catches his shrieks in cups of gold.*

Peggy Guggenheim has experienced—perhaps even enjoyed—a contested reputation in the many writings about her life, including her own memoir, which she revised and republished numerous times. Whether or not sponsoring such an exodus served her own self-interest, Peggy deserves respect for helping numerous artists and intellectuals to flee Europe before the Second World War. In actuality, Peggy shepherded most of them to New York City, where they enjoyed her patronage and friendship. In this book, the artists are brought instead to a resort in the jungle of western Mexico.

Costalegre means the coast of joy, and it's the actual name of the Pacific coastline that runs along the Mexican state of Jalisco. The resort that the artists are staying in is based on a place named Costa Careyes that still exists today. It's a strange, inspiring location that isn't easy to access for both geographical and financial reasons, and I will always be grateful to Daniele Ruais for opening her home to my family so that I could write this book.

Likewise, Jimmy Giebeler showed me a side of Careyes that I hadn't known before, and encouraged me—perhaps without even realizing he was doing so—to make my characters artists. Felix Martinez, Eddy Martinez, Jomy Rosa, Alison Patricelli, Luis and Marcy Mejia gave me the confidence and stamina to see this project through by distracting me with sport, and Hilda Rueda has been nothing but good humored throughout my efforts to learn Spanish. To my friends in Careyes—Marco, Monica, and Melanie especially—I've loved every *tope* of this wild ride.

My beloved daughter, with her kindness and her humor, inspires me daily not to screw this motherhood thing up, and Diego, I would not have been able to sink into this book as deeply as I needed to if it weren't for your support, your tejón-chasing skills, your love.

I must thank Rebecca Gradinger, whose mind was full of inverted question marks when I first shared this project with her. You said that you would follow me, and you did, and not every agent would do that, and that is why you are a cherished friend.

Masie Cochran, I knew I'd found my heart's editor when you told me that you had a lot of questions, but you didn't want any of them answered. I am a privileged writer indeed to be on this book's ship with you.

Also at Tin House: Anne Horowitz and Allison Dubinsky, thank you for your time, patience, and artistry as I defended Lara's syntax. Magic makers Nanci, Molly, Sabrina, Yashwina, Tony, Elizabeth, Alana, Jeremy, Miriam, and Morgan: thank you for believing in this book. And thank you, Miranda Sofroniou and Diane Chonette, for the perfect cover.

At Fletcher & Co.: Veronica, you're an herbal tranquilizer for my neurotic soul. Melissa, thank you in a variety of languages. Dearest Sophie Troff, merci.

Dasha, a true artist and my imagination's translator: your talent is as infinite as your generosity.

Pegeen: Your story wasn't told much. I hope you forgive me for giving it a try.